THE DALAI LAMA'S SMILE

PAULA CLOSSON BUCK

THE
DALAI LAMA'S
SMILE

stories

CINCINNATI 2025

Acre Books is made possible by the support of the Robert and Adele Schiff Foundation and the Department of English at the University of Cincinnati.

Copyright © 2025 by Paula Closson Buck
All rights reserved
Printed in the United States of America

Designed by Barbara Neely Bourgoyne
Cover art: images from Unsplash

ISBN-13 (pbk): 978-1-946724-85-4
ISBN-13 (ebook): 978-1-946724-86-1

No part of this work may be reproduced or transmitted in any form or by any means, electronic or mechanical, including photocopying and recording, or by any information storage or retrieval system, without express written permission, except in the case of brief quotations embodied in critical articles and reviews.

These stories are works of fiction. Names, characters, businesses, places, events, and incidents are either products of the author's imagination or used in a fictitious manner. Any resemblance to actual persons, living or dead, or actual events is purely coincidental.

The press is based at the University of Cincinnati, Department of English and Comparative Literature, McMicken Hall, Room 248, PO Box 210069, Cincinnati, OH, 45221–0069.

www.acre-books.com

Acre Books books may be purchased at a discount for educational use.
For information please email business@acre-books.com.

Contents

The Dalai Lama's Smile / 1

Deliquescence / 23

The Intervention / 45

Vertigo / 55

The Girl Who Loved Boyan Slat / 73

The Slight / 91

Feminine Mystique / 103

The Inventories / 123

Acknowledgments / 143

THE DALAI LAMA'S SMILE

The Dalai Lama's Smile

Morris receives his Christmas card nearly two weeks after what happened. The note from his son, Toby, says that work with the Tibetan monks is going well; it says the spirit of Christmas is still with him. What does it mean, *still*? Christmas hadn't come yet, and it would not come for Toby. When Morris's sister received her card, she said she thought of the Dalai Lama padding barefoot around his temple and about his devotees who loved him better than Jesus. The card that Morris's ex-wife received said that turkey was the only meat Toby missed. She is almost sure that, in spite of being a Catholic genetically, her son had gone native.

Morris's card is unsigned, and it ends midsentence. Since the other cards were finished, he figures he was most likely below Toby's mother and aunt on the list of people Toby would write to. He won't let that trouble him under the circumstances. But the card, sent anyhow and displayed on the mantel, does trouble Morris. It won't let him rest—not while he sits on the couch, the dog on his feet; not when he goes out walking past the defunct smokestacks of the furniture factory and the wintered-over marsh.

At night, when he comes back into the house and leaves his boots by the door, he glances up at the Christmas card on the way into the dining room. The face of the virgin is so pale and oblivious it seems to moon him. What his son said (Morris doesn't need to see it again) was "I don't think you know—" and there it ended.

Now, sitting on the wrong bus in a country of dark-skinned people, a bus that will apparently take seven or eight or ten hours to get there rather than the two or three he'd anticipated, he is going to find out what was so unknown to him. He will find the mark the boy left on that part of India that was somehow—how was that?— more like Tibet.

By the time he reaches the village, it is dark and he is nauseous, not so much from the curving road as from the acrid smell of the woman sitting next to him. She has wretched out the window twice, but the vomit smell is not enough to cover the body odor he's certain is hers, though he, too, has been traveling for days. Morris has, folded in his shirt pocket, a piece of the envelope with the name and address of the home for children where his son volunteered. It is written in his son's hand. Morris would have copied it but was afraid he would get it wrong. He wanted very much this time not to get it wrong.

He'd had one chance with his son—twenty-two years long— and what was it he did not know? In the Indian countryside, from the window of the bus, he'd seen old men nearly naked, rinsing their faces at dawn. He'd seen men asleep on small mountains of cauliflower, a boy rolling a tire in the morning mist. He'd seen a dead bull bloated in the heat at a crossing. All are things he had not known were in the world.

The smell of curry makes him want to vomit. The thought of the dead bull too. And the way the woman who was sick wipes her mouth with a tissue. Morris doesn't offer her water, though he has some. What he knows of his son has nothing to do with this place.

At one time, he had wanted the boy to know how things worked. They had taken apart more than one toaster and a transistor radio, which Toby had laughed at. Obsolete. And also, once, a lawn mower engine. With all that knowledge of working parts—which on first backward glance it seemed might have been useful in a country like this one—the boy had taken a shine to computers and (it hurt all over again to admit) gone to work with a charity. Did that make Toby a martyr now? He had told Morris, "It's only an internship." But as it turned out, it wasn't. It was the rest of his life. The only thing Morris knows will make him feel better is to understand the meaning of that. Charity is nuns in habits. Mother Teresa. What you do with what is left over. Surplus. The short end of the stick. To Morris, being Catholic means that you wear a St. Christopher medal to keep you safe.

Morris awakens to a dull sky and a disturbed sense of time. It might be early morning or dusk. When he stands up, he feels dizzy. It has been hours since he's eaten anything. Maybe even a day. Ambivalent clouds hang low over the mountains. Morris has not thought about how to conduct his business here. The journey has required all of his resources—his will, his money, his scant knowledge of the internet. He misbooked the trip once and only after a long harangue with someone at the airline managed to repair that damage. What had he thought would happen once he arrived?

Carrying the envelope that bears Toby's return address, Morris leaves the hotel and wanders into the town, past the bony asses of cows and the sign-laden restaurants and language schools stacked at the roadside. "First time to India?" a man says expressively when shown the envelope. But Morris is already thinking about whether or not the question is a trick. He moves on in search of the disinterested stranger who will simply point the way. Then, almost before he is ready, he finds himself in front of a doorway with a sign that says Himalaya Peace Home. To the maroon-robed monk who greets him at the desk inside he says, "I am Toby's father. Do you speak English?"

The monk, making a slight bow, says, "*Namaste*. Someone is expecting you?"

"No," Morris says, "probably not."

The monk looks uneasy. "I am sorry, Mr. Toby, for you," he says. "Sorry for the killing." He says this as if he himself were responsible.

Morris clears his throat and then reaches out and strokes the little ruffled curtain at the window before dropping his hand again to his side.

"You have come for the personal effect?" the monk says, wrinkles at the corners of his eyes emanating kindness.

Morris first takes this to mean that the monk thinks he is trying to achieve some kind of intimacy—with whom, he is not certain. But when the monk tells him there is a box of things at the monastery where Toby stayed, he feels his mission as understood by the monk diminished. "May I ask," he says, "what my son did here? I mean, what sort of place is this?"

"He made a website for us. And he maintained our database of donors. Those were his unique responsibilities," the monk says.

Morris nods. "Is that all?" he says, not really trying to mask his disappointment.

The monk looks at him with forbearance. A smile. "Toby was great in the hearts of all at Peace Home. To us, this work was of much important. It made possible that we sustain the children."

But Morris is thinking that if there were any beauty to the internet it was that you could maintain a website for an organization in Dharamshala from a place like Farmington or Dubuque. Virtual reality, wasn't that it? Even he understood that the computer was not the kind of machine you could get a limb tangled up in. Not the sort of thing you'd go to a third-world country and lose your life for. "Please tell me," he says, "that he ladled soup or distributed clothing. Tell me he taught people hygiene. Is this a Catholic organization? I don't fully understand."

The monk explains that it was started by a Catholic priest but is now a cooperative effort with a few Tibetans. He himself is the director. "Come in," the monk says, gesturing to the room adjacent. In the corner of an otherwise bare space, two young Indian boys sit on the floor in front of a Paleolithic television set. It takes a moment for Morris to register the face on the screen, and he thinks that surely his own mind must be playing tricks on him. "These boys we give an opportunity," the monk says with a humble sort of satisfaction.

"To watch *Mr. Bean?*" Morris says. It is the episode in which the ridiculous Mr. Bean is singing in church, mouthing the words he doesn't know and singing the *hallelujahs* loudly. Toby showed it to Morris once when he came to stay for the weekend.

"Yes, and also to attend school. They are Gujarati children. You know about the earthquake?" Morris's eyes are fixed on the screen, where, unable to find a handkerchief, Mr. Bean blows his nose into his suit coat pocket. Bored by the sermon, he is falling asleep on the man sitting next to him in church.

"And my son worked with these boys?" Morris says finally, wondering how he would possibly know about an earthquake in a place called Gujarati.

"This was the program of Toby. He taught the children to laugh again."

So far, what Morris is learning is of no comfort. He knew his son had wasted huge amounts of time on the computer, not to mention TV by way of the computer. So this was Toby's version of saving the world? Morris is caving in under the weight of his grief, which he had hoped might be lifted ever so slightly by knowledge of the good Toby had done. He has nothing to say.

When he leaves, the monk calls down the street after him from the doorway, "Mr. Toby, please! You are welcome!" Has he forgotten to say thank you? Gratitude is not an emotion available to him at the moment.

*

The last time Morris saw Toby, they had argued. He'd been working in the shop attached to the garage and Toby said, gesturing to the small engines, the fans and the fenders, the dishpans of used oil and the coffee cans full of bolts, "Your world is small. I'm sorry to say it, Dad, but it's made of parts that fit together to form machines no one really wants anymore."

"But everyone needs," Morris said.

"You don't know what need is," Toby said.

"And you do? At twenty-one, you know?" Morris kept to himself the thought that having a passport didn't make you a sage.

"I've seen things you wouldn't believe," Toby said, his shaggy hair obscuring his eyes. "Children who have been blinded so they'll get more sympathy from foreigners."

"So you're giving it to them." Morris looked at his boy hard. "I thank God daily that I don't have to live that way," he said. "I've worked my whole life so you wouldn't have to either." In the silence that followed, they both looked at the old Electrolux tank and wand that sat between them on the shop floor. "I'm contented with the life I have," Morris continued. Indicating the vacuum cleaner, he went on. "They don't make machines like that anymore. It's not magic, but I'm giving it an afterlife."

"Contentment is not the higher road," the boy had said.

"You go ahead and take that high road," Morris told him. "I've got an engine to repair."

The road Morris follows away from town when he leaves the charity leads past a few parked autorickshaws and taxis. Drivers loiter at the shoulder, talking on cell phones. After walking a short distance, Morris is blindsided by a little white sign that reads *St. John in the Wilderness*. He had not planned to go to that place. He stumbles into a grove of trees behind some Nordic-looking tourists who, having parked in the dirt lot, traverse the small rise on the other side of which sits the little white church. The site can only be described as idyllic—quaint and aromatic with pine. This is where Toby's high road had led. Had he sat inside to meditate? Had he chosen the place for religious reasons?

Morris overhears one of the blond teenagers saying he heard the body was found in the ditch. "Whoever did it dragged him over there." The kid seems to know more than Morris does. When the kid wonders aloud who the victim was, Morris walks away from the group, trying desperately to take in the peace of the place, the beauty of it as it was known to his son, but the fact of what happened silences the impressions that once might have come to either of them through the dappled sunlight. It's a gag Morris wants to stuff into the mouths of these vacationers. These voyeurs. People who still believe the world a place worth seeing.

Morris sees a gully on the northeast corner of the lot where the kid pointed, but he does not go over to look. Nor does he linger on the steps of the chapel, where Toby might have sat thinking about how little he, Morris, knew. *I don't think you know . . .* About what? All the ways he thought Morris had failed him? About love and how it worked or didn't work? Morris has the terrible feeling that he has forgotten something very important he was just about to say and it will never come back.

By late afternoon he is eating momos, the only thing on the menu he would even attempt to pronounce, in a restaurant at the center of town, the one with the neon, and feeling so exhausted he might pass out in his soup.

On the second day, the hotel sends up tea in the late morning, and the kid who brings it lingers in the room after he has set it on the table by the window. He is ratty looking, his pants too long and frayed at the heel of his running shoes. He seems to want to talk, but Morris doesn't, which he indicates by walking toward the door. He holds it open. Refusing to be ushered out, the kid—not a kid, really, on closer inspection, but maybe in his twenties—asks Morris, "Where you are going today?"

"No place now," Morris says. "I'm tired."

"But just before, where you are going?"

"The chapel," Morris says, standing awkwardly near because the tea guy has not moved. He gives the easiest answer, one he hopes needs no explanation.

"I am Bandhu," the guy says. "You are from America?"

"I won't need anything else, thank you," Morris says dismissively.

"And you are going to the charity? Peace Home?" the guy insists.

Morris says, "OK then, yes. You must have seen me. So why do you ask?"

The guy shrugs. "I am warning to you take care," he says. "There is bad feeling about Westerners." Though his expression is alert and eager, he does not look at Morris squarely when he speaks.

"Did you know the boy who was murdered?" Morris asks, studying him.

Bondo or Bandit or whoever he is walks back over to the tray and rearranges the spoon on the napkin. After a protracted pause, he says nervously, "I saw his name in the paper. Same surname to your passport."

That afternoon, Morris walks out to the edge of the upper village, the eastern side, where the Dalai Lama is said to live. Prayer flags strung in the trees look at first glance like the toilet paper some high school kids had used on the crab apple trees in his and Toby's yard one spring. You couldn't take it down really. You had to leave it to weather, and after the first rain it looked like used toilet paper, which was worse. Everyone saw that you had been singled out. "So what are you going to do about it?" Morris had asked Toby over breakfast the next day.

"What do you suggest?" Toby had said, his sarcasm succinct. He had been sullen that morning. Morris was sure Toby knew the kids who did it, and that it wasn't a friendly prank.

"Stand up for yourself—I can't say how. I'll leave you to work out the details." But Toby had merely gone out less, retreated further into the computer.

Now it seemed as if the boy had returned willingly to the scene of that humiliation. What did people see in these little scraps of longing or ignorance? They flapped, making the sky itself look ragged. Had Toby given in to that cosmic put-down Buddhism was? It sickened Morris to think of it. He had seen a picture of the Dalai Lama in a magazine on the airplane, and the man—or was he supposed to be a god?—was laughing. As if the universe were one big cosmic joke. What was so funny Morris failed to see. Maybe Toby could have told him.

Morris's grief works like a set of gears in his chest. In the morning, he is always aware that they have been turning at night. The mechanism is fueled not only by every memory of the difference between him and Toby but by every ordinary thing he now does that his son will not do again. Things they once might have had in common. Morris lifts the tea to his mouth, and Toby will not drink again. From the balcony, Morris watches a sparrow splash in a mudhole. It rained last night, and the air is cool. He argues with the proprietor of the hotel about the cost of the room just to hear the proprietor argue back. He wants Toby to argue with him now. To tell him he's the one who has wasted his life. To ask if it ever occurs to him to change his T-shirt. Why, when he'll just get more grease on it anyhow? But Toby does not argue. For the trip, Morris went to Kmart and purchased a six-pack of colored pocket tees. Each morning, he puts on a fresh one and sits a few minutes on the edge of the bed before he goes out, as if waiting for the boy to notice. It doesn't show, but under the shirt, the grief gears turn. Is it that or the altitude that constricts his breathing and makes it difficult for him to walk the road into town? A clean engine doesn't labor. He knows that. It's an engine running on sludge that labors.

At the police station, Morris is told little more than was related by the local officials back in Missouri and by the kid at the chapel. His son was found in a ditch on the grounds of St. John in the Wilderness, where he was known to have gone when he wanted to spend time alone. But there is one other thing. The officer tells him now that friends say Toby had gone to write Christmas cards, though none were found.

Morris doesn't know why he says nothing in response to this information, except that, at the moment, the card he received feels like the only thing that is between him and Toby alone. Even Toby's body has become mere evidence in a crime. Cause of death: blunt trauma to the head. Suspects: none, though Kashmiris have been indicted in the murders of other Westerners near Dharamshala, so the investigation is looking in that direction. His son did not appear to have been robbed. Several people who saw him shortly beforehand are being called for questioning. Unable to release further details at present. Will contact Morris—or rather the boy's mother, since she is listed as next of kin—when they have more information. Morris doesn't know why he even bothered making the trip to the police station since he doesn't press his case. He has always been the backup parent. He had accepted that status. And the distance from his son.

The hotel employee, who is lurking near the station, does not greet Morris when he comes out but moves to catch up with him when Morris walks past. Morris stops in the middle of the potholed street. "What do you want?" he says, making it clear he would prefer not to be followed.

Adopting a casual air and somehow, at the same time, an air of authority, the guy—was it Bondo?—says, "What did they tell you?"

"Nothing," Morris lies.

"As I thought."

"So what do you want?" Morris says, waving a fly away from the other man's mouth, as if hoping for less interference in their communication. Because it seems that what this man reveals to him is always vague and buzzing with unstated meaning. "What did you say your name was, anyway?" he says.

"Bandhu. Listen. There is a suspect. But the police, they don't know."

For a moment the grief gears in Morris's chest grind to a halt, and he thinks he might fall down. He does not trust Bandhu much generally, but what else does he have to go on? "How do you know that?" he asks.

"People are saying."

"So what?" Morris says, only half as a question, because he is not sure that he wants to know, and he also is aware now that he himself is concealing evidence. He might appear somehow guilty.

Bandhu shrugs. He then concedes, somewhat reluctantly. "Come. I show you something."

Through the village, Morris follows the sloppy hotel employee into whose hands he has, for reasons he does not understand, entrusted himself. He ponders what might happen to him in the next few minutes. Not knowing makes the world a vile place. Blessed are the peacemakers, for they will be bludgeoned anonymously. Dear God. Not knowing is the nightmare he's been living. And knowing?

How would that be? Would the world be a better place if there were someone to blame? Some terribly flawed logic at work in the brain of a maniac? A set of circumstances, at least?

"See that house there?" Bandhu says, interrupting his thoughts. They stop in front of a two-story house with a chalet-style roof and a balcony across the front. "In this house some years ago is living a priest. German. He is doing charity among the Indian people and the Tibetans too." Bandhu contemplates the vines growing up around the front window and onto the balcony. "He come here with very great ideas to help these people. There was living many orphans in this part."

Morris is certain of one thing. He does not want to hear about charity and its meaning for the poor. He should have simply asked who the suspect was before he allowed himself to be led on a historic tour of town. He shifts uncomfortably and digs at the linings of his pants pockets. The sky is dense with clouds that seem to have no intention of producing rain. "Did my son know this priest?" he says.

"No," Bandhu answers. "The priest, he died a few years prior. He is falling down the stair in this house. Is striking to the head."

"And the orphans?"

"This priest, he has to live with him two Indian boys who not have parents."

"A sad story," Morris says, because it seems like that must be the point of it, not because he can imagine any sadness relevant to his own.

"Yeah." Bandhu's mouth tenses then twitches with suppressed emotion. "Yeah," he says again. "We go back now. I make for you the tea. I must go for working." He turns and begins walking toward town, leaving Morris in front of the house, which appears empty until someone emerges at the back and dumps a tin of scraps for the chickens penned there. Walking quickly to catch up with Bandhu, Morris says, "It was an accident, right?"

"Who knows?" Bandhu says, distant. He continues to walk, and Morris follows him, afraid now to lose him. Closer to the center of town, they are absorbed into the weave of foot traffic. Huge bundles of branches, beneath which Morris can see only legs, are coming toward them on the road. A group of Indian tourists wrapped in god-awful color combinations—purple and orange and pink—make Morris wonder if he might have begun to hallucinate. He stops abruptly, grabbing Bandhu by the arm because they both seem in danger of disappearing into the strangers speaking psychedelic nonsense. "What are people saying?" Morris demands.

Bandhu pulls away but doesn't move on. "They are remembering," he says, "it was for the priest same kind of head injury to your son."

Morris takes a moment to process this. Same head injury. Maybe the priest didn't die from the fall? Toby and this priest were murdered by the same person? "And the suspect?" Morris says.

Bandhu is impassive. "Confidential," he says.

"Tell me," Morris insists, now wanting—yes, needing—to know.

Bandhu studies Morris's face, as if looking there for something he himself has lost. "One of the boys," he says.

"Why would he do something like that? One of the adopted boys? How old?"

"What the Father force him to do for so many years. That is the reason he might do." Allowing this information to sink in, Bandhu says, "Listen to me. Even when people suspect who kills the priest, they know that priest is deserving what comes to him. They see that to the boy he has made great damages, and they are not blaming the boy. Until now, they not *openly* suspect nothing. Until now. But now, they have concern."

"What do you mean, *concern*?" Morris says. "What are they talking about? I don't see the connection. Between my son and this so-called priest."

"Never mind," Bandhu says. Apparently frustrated with Morris's failure to grasp the situation, and quite possibly thinking better of what he has told Morris, he disappears into the hallucination of street life.

Morris sits down on the curb with his head in his hands. Why Toby? Was Toby a homosexual? The toilet paper in the trees was never a prayer for peace—he'd always known that much. His gut churns, and he vomits in the street. Because if he thought before that the work his son had done was meaningless, he knows now that all of it was a complete fraud. Priests pretending to care for the people they abused. Had Toby's life been sacrificed to such a scheme? Whoever or whatever Toby was, Morris is certain he would not have hurt anyone.

The box of Toby's personal effects offers little in the way of illumination. What astonishes Morris is how few possessions his son had in India. Some underwear, laundered and folded. Two pairs of jeans and a few T-shirts. A computer. An iPod. Two books: one called *Life of Pi* and one on meditation techniques. Morris stands on one side of a Formica reception counter in the monastery where Toby had been rooming. The place resembles a Howard Johnson's with its orange woodwork and its dated turquoise carpet. "Why was my son living here?" he asks the monk on the other side of the counter. "Had he become a monk, or is this some kind of hotel?"

"Your son was a spiritual man," the monk says, "but no, not a monk." Watching Morris finger the contents of his son's life absently, he says, "Toby understood that the material world is illusory. Things matter very little. What gets in our way is the desire we feel for them."

"I don't care about these things either," Morris says, suddenly angry, his face flushing with what he feels is an insult. "I do not desire these things." He closes the box in sudden disgust. "What I desire," he says in syllables dealt carefully across the counter, "is to know what happened to my son and why. And *illusory*. What does that mean? Here's what's left of Toby," he shouts. "This is all!" He lifts the box and then slams it on the countertop and shoves it at the monk. "I seem to have had a son a month ago. Now I seem not to have a son. Where did he go? How is it that in this land of peaceful grins and hospitality there exists such violence? Such corruption? Such hatred?" All of the indignation he might have expressed at the police station or at Bandhu surges through him.

Taking the assault in stride, the monk says, evenly, "It is that which we believe about the world that matters. The condition of the heart and mind directing our actions. We say in Tibetan Buddhism one must practice contempt for the world. The truth is what one carries inside him—into this world and again out."

"Oh, don't worry yourself about that," Morris says. "I have contempt all right. I hate this place. I hate that Toby ever came here to participate in your droning vegetarian ecstasies. The illusion is this serene charm of yours. I hate the lies that are passed around by religious fanatics—even well-meaning ones such as yourself. The priests and the monks and all the queer-assed mystics in this world."

The monk closes the box quietly, its four flaps forming a neat cross on top. "I am sorry. I know you are now breaking," the monk says.

Now breaking. Yes. Morris is. He wants to break others too. He wants them to give up the pretty pretense of sanity. Morris grabs the box before descending the staircase. He hopes he might stumble and go the way of the child-molesting priest. All the way down. He is being pushed. In this strange place, he feels more alone than he did even at Toby's funeral. More alone than when he first heard the news. What was the Dalai Lama doing at that moment? Shuffling in his soft slippers across some wooden floor, thinking thoughts of peace?

Exhausted and ashamed, not knowing where else to go, Morris walks back across town and out to the house where the hotel employee took him earlier. As he walks, he picks up a handful of cinders from the roadside and throws them into the air above his own head, feeling them rain down on him. Arriving at the house, he grabs a fist-sized stone and lobs it at the window above the balcony. There is satisfaction in the sound of shattering glass, and he picks up another stone. His arm cocked, he hears a voice shouting. Standing at the door is the woman he saw throwing scraps to the chickens the day before. "Hey, stop! What you are doing?" she says.

Morris lowers his arm. There is no logic to his vengeful pursuit. But he will not, like all the rest, turn a blind eye to a dead man's heinous behavior.

"Why you throw stone at Bandhu house? You make rain to come in!"

Bandhu house?

"Bandhu lives here?" he says aloud. He had thought, really, that no one lived there. Though he couldn't have explained the chickens.

Back in the room, Morris throws himself onto the bed and tries to sleep though it's only two in the afternoon, but next door, someone is droning. On it goes, some Zen kind of torment. The perfect accompaniment to the question *Which brother is Bandhu?* Morris can't stop thinking that, in this place, he may have been drinking tea courtesy of his son's murderer. He gets up and, digging through the box of Toby's things, he locates the little earplugs he saw in there earlier. They're not earplugs, really, but earphones, meant to be wired to something. They will work for what he needs. He puts them in to dull the sound, and still he tosses and turns for an hour or so, wondering if he should go to the police. He seems to be finding out things the police have failed to discover. Or have discovered but are keeping quiet. He gets up and calls for tea instead, but no one appears.

Not knowing: preferable, it seems, to knowing. Knowing things seems merely to give his anger a foothold. It brings strangers with faces and ill-fitting clothes into intimate relationship with Toby. He wants the boy to be left alone now, not to be embroiled in someone else's sick story.

Morris feels suddenly that he needs to get out of Dharamshala. He's been there only three days, but each day has served only to mock Toby's life. He begins, impulsively, to pile his T-shirts, mostly dirty already, into the duffel bag he brought. He digs through the box of Toby's things and takes out first the iPod, which he puts in his coat pocket, and then the computer and the charger, which he wraps in a sweater and stuffs into the duffel bag along with the rest of his clothes. There is a knock on the door, and he goes to open it. It's Bandhu, looking very nervous with a pot of tea and one glass. Morris lets him stand there uncomfortably as he tries to recall why he called him in the first place. "Forget it. No tea. I'm leaving," he says.

Bandhu attempts to set the tray down in the hallway, but he tips it and the tea spills at Morris's feet, where it darkens into a puddle on the carpet. "I know you are thinking I do the terrible things," he says.

"Look," Morris says. "Don't make your confessions to me. That's what the police are for. I don't want to see you."

Bandhu looks devastated. "Please," he says. "My brother is not correct in the head. In the heart, he is destroyed by the priest. Our father. And Toby, he is saying always kindest glories of praise for this man who my brother hate. To the website your Toby is writing tributes. He not knowing nothing about what is happening years ago."

Morris sits back down on the bed beside the duffel bag. "What is the date today?" he asks.

"Twenty-four December," Bandhu says officiously, returning to his role as hotel bellboy, as if they had not been talking about anything murderous. "No. Wait. Is twenty-five."

"The police never saw the Christmas cards," Morris says.

"I know," Bandhu says sadly.

"But I saw them. Mine was unfinished."

"Yes."

"You were getting rid of the evidence. Protecting your brother? Or yourself. Why didn't you just destroy them?"

"I thought you and the others would want them."

"To brighten our holidays, I suppose," Morris says. "Why do you tell me what you have not told the police?"

"I love my brother. But after I send the cards, I am thinking of the people who are receiving them. And then you come here to my hotel of work. Looking for your son. You are a good father," Bandhu says. Morris can see that Bandhu speaks of these things not without agony. "You want I am telling the police?" Bandhu says with resignation.

"Maybe you're wrong about everything," Morris says.

What Morris feels for his son is mostly anger and hurt and regret and wishfulness. That doesn't make him the best of fathers. Now that he has the general idea, he is certain it doesn't much matter to him anymore who killed his son. It matters only that his son was deluded in his compassion. Sucked into a sham operation. That he played a role in a pedophile's dream. The solutions are coming, but to the wrong problem. He wants now, more than anything, to separate Toby in his memory from all of this.

Against Morris's wishes, Bandhu drags the duffel bag and the cardboard box, too, down the steps to the lobby of the hotel, leaving the teapot overturned in the hallway. Morris takes the duffel bag from him without a word and, resignedly, hoists the box he had meant to leave onto his own shoulder. He moves alone down the road toward town, not looking back, stumbling into potholes and over ruts. At the bus stop, he boards an idling bus without asking its destination.

Inside, the bus is already crowded with backpackers, Tibetans, and Kashmiris. There isn't much choice in seats. Morris makes his way to the back then climbs over the knees of a plump monk in a red robe. The monk's arms, bundled in a fleece jacket, spill over onto the soaking wet seat beside him. The window is stuck open. It's getting cold, and Morris inhales diesel fumes as the bus lurches forward and begins to heave them gently from side to side on the sinuous mountain descent.

When Morris opens a tin of Altoids to prevent almost certain nausea, the monk, not looking at him, extends a flat palm to receive the mint Morris has not offered. Morris looks out the window as if he doesn't understand. He pulls the earphones out of his pocket and puts them in, then plugs them into the iPod from his coat. Only on second thought does he try pressing the button, finding his way in. Toby always said it was easy. Intuitive. The song he hears is about an electric bird. It is searingly clear, and the acoustics fill Morris's head. He wonders how the sound is received. Or stored in the little device. Where it comes from. He watches out the window, tired and cold and beginning to let go. This is Toby's channel. It's coming from somewhere far beyond the moment. Morris feels riddled with the music.

The monk's eyes are closed now and his shaved head lolls dangerously close to Morris's shoulder. They pass through lower Dharamshala and then, in view of one of the rattiest slums Morris has seen, the tent city below the town, the driver pulls over and opens the door. No passengers come on board, and the others wait without any sense of expectation. The settlement looks postapocalyptic. Like what's left after every violence has been done, the infrastructure ravaged, the people just plain too exhausted to wonder what will happen next. The tents are low, inverted Vs of black plastic. Here and there, smoke rises from a cooking fire. Some children stand close to the road, looking at the bus. An old man with a bucket is making his way amid the tents as if he were off to collect something. Or maybe to deliver something. Morris follows the man's progress across the lot with curiosity until the man stops abruptly and lifts his tunic to squat, exposing a bony ass. Morris can't help staring. Nothing else is moving but the man, who uses his hand and the water in the bucket to rinse himself unabashedly.

It feels to Morris as though he has been singled out for some dark cosmic joke. He searches for the compassion his son felt for these people. What comes over him is, instead, a feeling of being exposed and humiliated in his grief, which is obscene—something ugly and terribly private that he must tend with the whole world looking on.

Toby had written a card thinking ahead to this day, a Christmas day beyond the end of his own life. Morris will have to live it without him. The card said *I don't think you know*, but maybe Morris does know. Maybe now he does.

And now the old man is carrying his bucket back across the wasteland, home. Unable to sit and wait for the totality of annihilation to take hold in him, Morris pushes past the knees of the monk and retrieves the box of Toby's belongings from the rack above the seats. He makes his way in small collisions along the aisle to the open door. He isn't at all sure what he will do, but he can't just sit there letting it all happen. Outside, the driver is talking to a guy who is doing some maintenance on the rear wheel of the bus. An icy snow is beginning to fall. Morris's arms and shoulders are tired already from hauling his stuff through town, and the box weighs more than what's left in it.

The kids who have been studying the repair operation from a few yards away are watching Morris now. A small, grubby one points to the box. Morris hesitates before he drops the box in the dirt, and they keep studying him.

He isn't aware of having given any signal when two gangly boys who look to be eleven or twelve spring forward suddenly and dig the cardboard flaps open. It's just as well. Unable to watch, he turns and walks back toward the bus.

Only when he reaches his seat again does he see from the open window a pair of bunched blue jeans galloping off into the dust alongside the orange T-shirt that reads *Catholic Charities*, and the lime green one that Morris remembers has a figure throwing a Frisbee and *Life is good* on the front—bits of Toby running off through the sleet in every direction.

Deliquescence

Kanela, the goat, has gnawed down all of the asphodel in the empty lot, so the bulbs now are fat knuckles exposed in the dirt. Daphne empties the wheelbarrow onto a heap of marble scrap. She's been cleaning out the studio; the students arrive today. Where she lives and works has never been a particularly pretty place. At the edge of town, theirs is one of a cluster of nondescript houses built in the seventies and eighties. That's why, on the studio brochures, they show what was once the ancient harbor across the coast road with its three broken columns. Not a lie, exactly.

Daphne lingers at the edge of the field, feeling like it's where she belongs—what's left of her between the winter's commissions and the summer's work of teaching.

"What're you doing out there?" Jess calls from the gravel access road between Daphne and the house. He's standing beside the old Toyota, still doing up his belt. Not waiting for an answer, he says, "I need to pick up Benny at the ferry after I drop the kids at school." The twins climb into the backseat with their daypacks. "Man, am I sore from digging holes," Jess says.

Jess has been planting trees with Daphne's old friend Nektarios, whose dream of reforesting the island is hopelessly idealistic, even with Jess's help. Nektarios, however, would return from a day spent planting to tell you all about softening the edges of the self, about taking one's place in the biosphere. Jess, on the other hand, grumbles about how much he hurts and how many of last year's trees have been sabotaged by goats. It's a discomfort he and Daphne can talk about.

Jess tries to open the car door on the driver's side, then kicks it. "Fucking hell," he mutters, going around to crawl through from the passenger side. The engine comes to life, and he makes a three-point turn then rolls down the window. "Just leave him to it, Daphne. How hard can it be?"

Him. That would be Benny. Daphne watches Jess pull away.

It's been a long time since she has done any of her own work, but the studio is still a sacred space for her, everyone tapping into the earth's benevolent ions. The first two years he came, Benny threatened an equilibrium she would do almost anything to preserve. Maybe Jess gets that, and maybe he doesn't. But at the mention of Benny, Daphne is all edges.

Almost without intention, she crosses the road to the pebbly beach. Nude bathing isn't permitted on account of the island's religious orthodoxy, but today she doesn't have time to go back to the house for her suit, and she doesn't care all that much either. Seeing no one, she drops her clothes and enters the sea, plunging quickly beneath the surface. She swims several long strokes before resurfacing. All of the bad washes away, all of the anxiety, time measured only by her own held breath. She stops to tread water and take in sea and sky, almost indistinguishable at the horizon. The profiles of landforms across the water are ancient familiars.

Too soon, the ferry from Piraeus pulls around the headland and into the new harbor, interrupting her view. Swimming back to shore, Daphne nearly runs into a large, gelatinous blob. She stands up, rowing away from it with her hands. It's a jellyfish. Not the smaller stinging kind. A Mediterranean jelly. She's seen them before, but never here. This one looks a bit grotesque at the surface, its dome a yellowish brown, though she knows their frilly underskirts can be beautiful when seen from underwater. Maybe the presence of this one has to do with climate change. Avoiding it, she makes her way to shore, slips back into her clothes, and hurries home to shower before Jess gets back with Benny.

The first year, Benny had come to the studio for two weeks. He was no artist, but he had some experience working in clay, and he thought the pomegranate he'd decided to sculpt in marble looked simple enough. Something his wife would appreciate. He'd shaped the clay maquette rather quickly in the first couple of days. By day three, he was learning to use the pointing device to establish the corresponding depths to which he would work the stone. But after the weekend, having removed only a small amount of material from the block he'd chosen, he'd begun to take frequent breaks. Rather than joining the others midmorning for coffee and sweets under the bougainvillea, he would walk out along the coast road toward town. He'd return two or three hours later and, dismayed by the heat and his lack of progress, would ask for Daphne's help. After lunch, he didn't come back at all.

"What's with Benny?" Daphne had said, stopping at his abandoned station one afternoon as she made her rounds of the students. It was quiet in the studio, except for the tapping of mallets on chisels. A stray cat sprang up onto the workbench, and Daphne shooed it away and out the door. Stefan, a veteran of the studio who worked next to Benny, made a dismissive shrug of the mouth. Who knew? He was setting points for translating to marble a clay sculpture he'd finished and exhibited back in Geneva. "I'll need you today," he said to Daphne. "Most of the afternoon."

Lola, a young Nigerian woman from London, stood working on

the other side of the tall industrial table. Seeing her raise an eyebrow at Stefan's demand, Daphne smiled almost imperceptibly. Though new to marble, Lola was a talented sculptor. Daphne found her cultural mash-ups between Cycladic and African fertility idols oddly powerful with their smooth, upturned moon faces and low-hanging, conical breasts. "Have *you* seen Benny lately?" Daphne asked her.

"Not around here," Lola said, intent on the maquette she was still shaping.

"Anywhere?" Daphne asked.

Lola said, "I've been here, working." She looked up at Daphne again. "There's a lot to do on this island if you're in search of distractions."

Benny showed up the next morning and moaned about how far behind he was. He said the pomegranate seemed reluctant to emerge from the stone. Daphne had talked a lot about not imposing a form on the marble but rather releasing one that somehow existed within it. One of the other students offered, "You have to get into the meditative rhythm of it, Benny. We wouldn't be doing this if the stone didn't resist us."

"It needs a kind of devotion," Daphne said, demonstrating, again, the technique of guiding the point chisel with one hand, allowing it to stutter across the surface of the stone. She held the hammer loosely to let its weight do the work.

That afternoon, returning from errands in the harbor, Jess spotted Benny at Café Meltemi across the plateia, sitting with his arm around a woman who wore sunglasses and a beach caftan. Though Benny pretended not to see him, Jess was sure he did. All of this Jess reported to Daphne when he got home.

"OK," Daphne said. "I won't be the judge of what he is doing. I'll give him what he is paying for. At least he is paying."

Payment *was* sometimes an issue. Stefan, from Geneva, and a woman named Agnes, from Munich, had both considered themselves personal friends after their first two-week stay at the studio and asked for a reduced tuition. For some reason, Jess, who managed correspondence and other administrative aspects of the studio, had agreed to it. To make matters worse, Stefan was arrogant and demanding of Daphne's time and expertise. He treated her not like a mentor, or even a fellow artist, but instead like a technician in a marble factory who would help execute his projects. Though she chafed a bit under it, Daphne withstood the humiliation.

Benny, on the other hand, had not asked for a reduction. By the end of the second week, Daphne was spending more time on the pomegranate than Benny was. Benny said that, in the interest of completion, he "felt comfortable" with her working on it, even if he wasn't there. He wanted something to take home.

Fixing a late meal of flatbreads with feta for Daphne and the children, Jess hacked a red pepper in two, making a loud *thunk* with the knife. "Now he's getting more than he paid for," he said.

Still, Daphne released the pomegranate with its beautiful, uneven contours and its delicate crown, allowing it the imperfections of both marble and fruit, though not those of Benny. In doing this, she remembered who she was or had been. Benny didn't make her who she was.

There had been a whole series of the pieces Daphne called *Ghost Leaves*: Chestnut. Mulberry. Pin oak. They called up forests cut down centuries before for agriculture or shipbuilding. Though sculpted from stone, Daphne's elegiac leaves gave the impression of lightness, as if they had just now fallen to the ground and might, at any moment, be picked up again by the wind. They'd been exhibited as an installation in Athens, arranged in rows like tentative grave markers. With that show, Daphne had begun to make a name for herself in the European art world. The only two unsold pieces were stored in the annex to the house. They were meant to be an inspiration to her, or at the very least, a tangible reminder of her accomplishment. But when she thought of them now, they served only as proof that she wasn't who she'd thought she would be. She'd have tried to sell them by now if she hadn't been afraid to find out they were now worthless—or at best, perhaps, the last things of value she would create.

As a child, Daphne had waited at home for her friend Nektarios to walk the two hours back to their village from the sculpting school he attended. Each day, he would teach her everything he had learned. Not terribly interested in the trade or the art, he felt he had little use for it otherwise. She had attended the school run by Ursuline nuns where girls went blind making lace. But she felt with her whole being that she was not a tablecloth-and-doily girl. Every stone in the terrace of her family's tiny house on the cliff facing the sea bore her bas-relief geckos and snails. Nektarios, on the other hand, loved trees, not stone. Even as a boy, he had believed that no one could keep him or Daphne from doing what they loved. "You can be the next famous sculptor from this village, and I will live like a chestnut tree," he told her. Dear Nektarios!

Sometimes Daphne wondered why she hadn't ended up with him. He had said once that she was better at being loved than at loving. He had said it, somehow, without judgment, only curiosity, as only Nektarios could.

Then she'd met Jess—an American vagabond slumming around the Greek islands. His devil-may-care charisma was grounded in an appreciation for art that he'd gained in a course he failed at college. He had followed her to the island after the big exhibition in Athens. He loved the idea of the simple life he believed was hers, built around the elemental sea and stone and sky. He loved her friend Nektarios and his moonlight eco-actions.

Daphne fell for Jess's candid disregard for whatever was expected of him. And as much as Jess liked surprising other people, he liked to surprise himself. When just weeks into their romance—the very week he was to go back home—she discovered she was pregnant, Daphne had been inclined to have an abortion, but Jess wanted the baby. The two babies, even, when the number became clear. Somehow, he convinced her that having twins with someone she hardly knew was a wonderfully spontaneous thing to do. Fertility would promote creativity. It was living dangerously! They married for his visa.

A year later, the economy collapsed, and all of Greece was caught in a tragic, slow-motion free fall. Without income, and reeling from the exhaustion of motherhood, Daphne had welcomed her first commission, which was part of a stimulus restoration grant from the EU. Jess took care of the babies. And somehow, the love between her and Jess grew—his incurable optimism taking the edge off their losses.

In the seven years since then, Daphne rarely allowed herself to indulge her disappointment in having accomplished nothing. But it was almost always there now, that ache that arose in her chest and lingered like a membrane between herself and everything that might make her feel real joy—even the children as she helped them with their schoolwork, or as they hung on her shoulders, listening while she and Jess sat in the garden with the students, discussing global politics or climate change, or arguing about who was the island's greatest sculptor. Jess, who had never stopped believing, said it would be her.

The second year Benny came to the studio, he was worried about disappointing his wife because she had loved last year's pomegranate so much. He proposed an elaborate bas-relief with a classical motif copied from a picture in his pocket. He seemed eager and excited, running his fingers back over his receding hairline and pacing the studio as he talked about a sense of connection to the ancients. Daphne, only a little bit wary, suggested he scale the project back and choose a detail to execute. He sketched a foot among acanthus leaves onto a marble tile small and light enough that he could easily carry it home.

The first morning, Daphne helped him identify the high and low points of his design. Before he left for the afternoon and didn't come back, Benny said, "Use mine to demonstrate. I'm not possessive!" He laughed happily, and that was the last Daphne saw of him until he turned up at the house one evening four days later.

"Do you think love is important?" he said, sitting at the big marble table in the garden and waiting for her to lay out the drinks and bakery sweets he could always count on.

She added water to the ouzo she had poured, turning it cloudy. Why would he even ask? She didn't want Benny to think she disapproved of his affair. After all, when she and Jess met, he was still supposedly with his American college sweetheart. They'd spent many a sultry afternoon in Daphne's bed. He would mail his girlfriend postcards of old women crawling the stone-paved hill to the church for penance. Daphne longed for those days. Not much happened in their bed anymore.

"It isn't the art that makes me happy," Benny said, running his hands back through his hair, as if trying hard to work something out in his head. "It's like art is the price I have to pay for being happy. I used to love it, sure. But it wasn't . . . It didn't change anything."

"This woman you're sleeping with, Benny, does that change something?"

"I'm like a new person," he said.

Daphne couldn't say that art had made her happy, though she had believed it would. Those days, art was only what might keep her from feeling like no one. Was the choice between art and love? Benny was, indeed, radiant. He held himself differently. His shoulders were broader. He had bought himself a black T-shirt with a European cut that didn't engulf him American style. "And when you go home? What are you like then?" she said.

"Relieved that she doesn't know. And that's only because I take her the marble." He leveled his gaze at Daphne. "Please."

"Why don't you just tell her?"

"I can't. This other thing is not sustainable year-round."

More than once in the days that followed, when Daphne was working at Benny's station, she looked up and caught Jess watching her from the doorway of the studio. He would turn and go without a word. "It's a teaching piece," she told the others. She used it to show them how to achieve an illusion of depth on a slab of marble just two centimeters thick, how to soften the jut of higher points, like the anklebone, with the riffler file. She would give the students what they needed. This was what Benny needed.

Which was different, it turned out, from what Jess needed. Jess failed to understand how Daphne could let herself be used like that.

"It's no skin off my neck," she said.

"Your back. No skin off your back."

"So you agree," she said.

"Daphne, I loved you because you believed in art. You thought people were at their best when they were working stone. Not when they were just fucking around and pretending to be working stone."

"*Loved* me, Jess?"

When he looked at her these days, there was no trace of the boyish smile that had been his, or of the sandy blond optimism that had always struck her as distinctly un-Greek. With his tree-planting and his nurturing of the children, his hands-off appreciation for art, he had always complemented her. And though she didn't want to admit it, she loved his devotion to her—not only as a woman but as a sculptor. That had gone out of his face lately too. When he looked at her now, she saw herself as nobody he could love.

"I make the coffee, update the website, take photos of your crazy students, drive them to the ferry! I send hundreds of emails all winter and spring, and I take the children to school. Then I bring them home and feed them, and once they're in bed, I try to soothe your damaged ego. I've given up everything for your art," he said, his mouth downturned with the effort of controlling his emotions.

It seemed to Daphne he was making a case not that he still loved her but rather that none of this had ever been OK. She felt the haphazard structures their love had built collapsing in the torrent of his disdain, which caught her by surprise.

"I gave up my art when I started teaching—and doing commissions—so that we wouldn't have to stop feeding the children. And you don't love me anymore now because I'm helping Benny with his foot?"

"You're letting a delusional little fuck from Indianapolis take credit for your work! You're helping him create a lie. Do you think the other students respect you for that? Do you think even Benny has an ounce of respect for you?"

"You're from Indianapolis, Jess."

"Shit, Daphne," he said.

That night when she lay against his backside, her hand low on his hip, his stillness made her feel like a lichen or a parasite, merely tolerated by a passive host. His breathing slowed and deepened, and at last she let the hot tears come.

All fall and winter of the second year, Daphne fed the hurt she felt into her work. Her commission piece was a new altar for an Orthodox church on Syros, and they wanted it ready for Easter. The tortured body, the weeping women. Everyone agreed about her role in the arrangement. They would pay her to carve the altarpiece to be used for the glory of a version of God she had disavowed—openly during her Ghost Leaves period and secretly long before. She would work tirelessly and would be acknowledged. Jess would not object. With each stroke of the chisel, each apostle's chin, each turn of the acanthus scrollwork, she felt a bitterness she could not dispel.

Jess couldn't forgive her for completing Benny's bas-relief. And she wouldn't apologize, because Jess had also begun to make her feel, in not-so-subtle ways, that not completing anything since the Ghost Leaves constituted utter failure on her part. "Why are you making this about me?" she asked him one night. Outside, the sea surged over the coast road, and the wind from the north howled around them, rattling the shutters.

"Because it's always about you, Daphne. Whether you're a success or depressed because you're not. Making art, or making everyone else miserable because you're not. It's always about you and what you're being deprived of. When has it ever really been about anyone but you?"

That seemed terribly unfair, considering the sacrifices she had made. Men could be tired and sore, but were women supposed to do it all with a smile? It was true that she needed Jess's easygoing lack of ambition. Had loved that about him. But maybe, just as much, he had needed her sense that all that was most beautiful was either hidden or just out of reach. And even her relentless desire to make that beauty visible.

It wasn't for lack of trying that Daphne hadn't finished anything new. Sometimes, while working on the commissions, she would steal an hour or two from the family or her sleep and she would bring in a hunk of new marble and try to find the beauty within it. But each time, she felt diminished by her earlier self, by some need to be brilliantly original. And she knew she could do nothing with scraps in an hour or two between the needs of others. She might never be worthy of her village of sculptors, or of the great, recondite beauty still in the marble, though she possessed the cruel gift of understanding just how much was hidden there. Her studio lay near the increasingly busy harbor road, and she breathed exhaust whenever an old pickup passed, or even when Jess returned in the rusted Toyota from town, where all winter he drank raki with the locals.

Nektarios called one evening to ask Daphne what was with Jess, who seemed to have lost interest in planting, but what could she tell him? "I don't know who I am anymore," she said.

Nektarios, who was becoming more and more like a chestnut tree, said, "Isn't that a good thing?"

"Do you think I'm selfish? Self-absorbed? Does wanting to make art make me selfish? Tell me, Nektarios. You know me better than anyone."

"Maybe a little bit, Daph," he said.

Having returned from the ferry, Benny and Jess are waiting in the garden when Daphne emerges from the house, her hair still damp. They are drinking the Greek coffee Jess has prepared. There are also two new students from Australia, and Lola has arrived from London. Agnes, who sculpts massive human limbs that seem to be in the process of emerging from rough-cut blocks of marble, steps out of the workshop and announces radiantly that last year's, the largest she has made so far, has inspired her to buy a house on the island. She can't part with the sculpture, and she can't send it home to Switzerland! Everyone cheers, and Daphne is happy to have the conversation taken up with Agnes's plans, though she can't help wondering why Agnes would need to negotiate a discounted rate for the studio if she can afford to buy a holiday house.

Daphne listens as the newly arrived students share their ideas. There's a lot of interest in vessels of various sorts this year, though Lola, who will stay most of the summer, wants to sculpt the head of an African/Greek goddess. Benny is thinking of some kind of fish. He isn't sure. "Are we good, Daphne?" he says, pulling her aside when the others go off to find their stations.

"Meaning . . . ?" She wants him to say what he is asking her to do.

"I'm asking as a friend, Daph. I don't want to waste even an hour of the time I have on this glorious island. Every hour I spend here with her adds years to my life." Daphne groans imperceptibly, wondering how many more years she is doomed to this role. In response to her silence, he says, "You should know that my marriage has gotten better, now that my wife believes in me."

All winter and spring, Daphne has tried to be more like Nektarios. He says ego is what separates us from the earth, separates her from the stone that she loves. It is a sort of existential clinginess. She wants to let go, however dangerous that might feel. Nektarios tells her it's different than giving up. And, as a teacher, Daphne has had some practice at this letting go. Over the past few years, she has sent bits of herself out to Sweden and South Africa, to Virginia and California and Quebec in the form of lopsided artichokes and smooth marble phalluses, in busts and epitaphs and lonely, unschooled fish.

She thinks about these things as she talks with Lola about how to work the tight curls in the hair of the Greco-African goddess.

Lately, Jess has been going out at night and drinking raki with the students up at the Windmill Bar, leaving her alone to put the children to bed. One night when they have gone, Daphne uses the outdoor shower to wash off the day's marble dust. She steps out from behind the teak privacy panels, wrapped in her towel, just in time to see a big, orange moon rising between the white cubes of the neighboring houses—and Lola, entering the courtyard from the studio, where she has once again stayed late, working.

Lola gazes at her in silence. "Will you show me your work? The Ghost Leaves?" she says. "I've been wanting to see them."

Daphne hesitates. It would cost her something to go there. "It's old work, Lola," she says.

"It's amazing work. I've seen the catalog. And it's still yours."

Daphne says with a laugh, "That makes it rare, doesn't it?" She believes that Lola truly admires her, and maybe she is desperate for admiration. Still dripping, she leads Lola to the neglected little annex attached to the house, and she feels for the key above the door.

Dust from the access road and the empty lot has infiltrated the room. At the back of the annex, past some large tins of olive oil and a broken beach umbrella, sit the two large sculptures—two leaves as big as washbasins or grave steles. Daphne runs a finger over the smooth, dust-coated marble of the first. Looking for a cloth to wipe the leaf clean, she attempts to open the wooden drawer of the table on which the pieces sit. The drawer sticks, so she uses both hands to shimmy it open. As she does, the towel she is wearing from the shower drops into a small puddle of water on the concrete floor. Somehow, she doesn't reach to pick it up.

She wants to be, if only for a moment, in that little Eden of two leaves.

Wants to stay clean and naked, and maybe to not be ashamed in front of Lola because, the night before, Jess, a little drunk in front of the others, had suggested that what she was doing for Benny made her "an art whore." What did that make him in his administrative role, he wanted to know. It was a humiliation far worse than anything Benny had ever made her feel.

And now Lola is standing close, her eyes wide in the long moment when Daphne leaves the towel on the floor. It's Lola who moves so that their bodies touch, tentatively. But it's Daphne who takes Lola's hand from her own shoulder and guides it to her breast, feeling a ripple of pleasure as Lola takes the nipple between her thumb and her forefinger. Feeling generally horny and rejected by Jess, Daphne is surprised by the unbidden pleasure of Lola's fingers inside her.

They are startled by a child in the doorway, up for a glass of water and calling for Daphne. Daphne snatches up her towel and guides the child into the kitchen, not looking back at Lola.

Two days later, on a Sunday, Jess has organized the whole group to go to a feast up in Daphne's village after the morning's work. The music is in full animation when they arrive, the impetuous fiddle and the guitar insistent in their circular melodies. The revolutions of the dancers widen and snake into themselves with an understated bobbing. It looks to Daphne as if an elegant human machine were stitching them to the earth, trying to mend the tear of daily living. When the music stops, they drop hands and cry out in happy fatigue. Some of them wander off to drink more retsina and rejoin conversations they had left.

Jess sits on a bench under the plane tree beside Benny and his beautiful Russian woman friend, whom Benny doesn't introduce when Daphne approaches and greets them. Daphne comments on the turnout; the locals have worked hard to make tourists feel welcome. She is uncomfortable at seeing Jess with Benny and the woman, who keeps putting her hand to her neck, as if she, too, were uneasy. Jess's sitting with Benny seems to say, "It's not him I have a problem with. It's you."

The other students pile their plates with grilled pork and lemon, and they settle onto the edge of the fountain across the plateia, the fountain with the fish that Daphne carved when she was just twenty-two. That seems like eons ago, when the village was proud of her.

Nektarios takes up the lead in the next dance. He dances like someone with a gift. He is taken by the music. His body moves in taut flourishes, his head thrown back in joy like some Bacchus, long curls flying. Whenever she sees him dance, Daphne understands something she has lost, some part of her spirit that cannot participate fully because she's always elsewhere. Always disappointed. Nektarios breaks the chain of dancers to pull her into the circle, and her feet know what to do.

As she circles past the plane tree, she sees Jess watching. She imagines him thinking, "Don't pretend for a minute you're anything like Nektarios." She has suspected for a while that Jess was jealous of their friendship.

Later, he finds her in the crowd and says, "You know, Daph, if you were the one having an affair, I wouldn't care so much. Those things happen, and maybe they're OK in the end. But you keep choosing to do the one thing that will make my life with you feel worthless." His sandy, straight hair falls across his forehead.

They wander down the pathway out of the plateia, gaze at the gleaming, moonlit Aegean far below. Jess stops and leans on the whitewashed wall of a house. "I've never been good at anything but making things possible for you," he says.

Daphne considers telling him what happened with Lola, to see if she can hurt him. Or she will tell him in order to keep her friendship with Nektarios in the clear. It's important for her that Nektarios continue to exist in the world of ideals.

But she feels for Jess, in that moment, a kind of sympathy. She touches the sleeve of his shirt. "No one can make you feel worthless, Jess. Not me or Benny or anyone." She lets her hand drop. "I can't give your life meaning. You're asking too much of me."

"So now I'm the one who's asking too much. And Benny—it's all in the course of a day's work? You're happy with what you're doing, I guess?"

Strangely, Daphne *is*. Strangely, in spite of everything, she feels it would be wrong to stop working on the piece for Benny. She believes it is quite possibly the most beautiful thing she has made so far.

She works on it while the other students are independently

busy. She works at night when she is restless, when one of the children has awakened her with a bad dream or an achy leg and she can't go back to sleep. She returns to bed in the early hours of the morning, and the whole thing seems to morph in her imagination while she sleeps. Her whole life morphs. She's working the orbit of the tawny veins in the marble in order to find the center, unleashing the movement in the stone. But now it matters not at all who she is or who will take credit for the making. All of the names and all of the ghosts of herself fall away. She feels, once again, the thrill of contraries, of something impossibly fluid emerging from something stubborn and difficult, of releasing primordial messages of beauty and unrelenting transience from deep inside the earth. While she is working, she feels an uncanny devotion to the moment.

The day she finishes, the others gather around her and applaud. The sculpture is wildly beautiful, they all agree. It has a fluid, marine quality, transforming as you circle it. Stefan says that, from where he stands, it looks like a sea creature. Lola says it resembles a vulva. Daphne feels her face flush. In leaving Lola very much alone since their encounter, she knows she is causing hurt. From the perspective of Jess, who has heard the commotion and come out to join them, the sculpture looks like a distorted human heart. The anatomical kind. But with a floating apron, or a fringe, if you step just a little bit to the right. And yet, they agree, it is none of these things. It possesses the gravity of a quarry mined for centuries and the weightlessness of floating in time.

"It's all you, Daphne," Jess says on his way out. He shakes his head. "I love that, but Benny's wife will never buy it."

When the others return to their work, Daphne pulls Lola into the garden and sits down opposite her at the marble table. "What you saw in the annex, Lola, that's a version of myself I . . . I won't go back to."

"You don't mean the leaves," says Lola.

"No, not just the leaves."

"So, what? We're talking about another lie you think is necessary?" Her back to the potted birds-of-paradise, Lola looks as sensuous and self-assured as a queen bee.

"No," Daphne says. "We're talking about the truth. I can't explain what happened, but it happened once." Daphne feels flimsy in her faded linen dress, wearing Jess's old button-down shirt as a smock over it—as if she were trying to cover something up. "I was coming apart in there, Lola. You took me to a vulnerable place, and I let you in."

"You did!" Lola says, earnest and taking hold of Daphne's wrist.

"But that's all," Daphne says. She pulls her hand away.

"Now you're finding out who you are. You're discovering the very source of your creative genius. It shows in the work! But you'll lie about that too?"

"I'm trying to let go and it's . . . dangerous to those around me. People who want me to be one thing or another."

"You have to insist on who you are. Anyone can see what's happening between you and Jess. And how you let Benny take advantage of you."

"I'm sorry, Lola. I was impulsive. And a little bit selfish. But you can't say or know what's happening for me. I'm sorry I hurt you."

Lola's dark eyes become impenetrable. Unforgiving. "Ignoring me was cruel enough. Sorry is worse."

Late that afternoon, Daphne and Jess walk with the twins out past the newer houses, the ones that have spoiled their view of the sea, and across the road to swim. The twins run ahead and cry out when they reach the pebbly beach. It's covered with jellyfish.

The jellies are in the water too, their amber-colored domes hovering above lacy, branched underskirts like stalks of cauliflower. The family has never seen so many jellies. On closer inspection, they can see that the underskirt is finished with a delicate ball-fringe of purply black nerves. The boy picks up a piece of dry cane and pokes at a blob on the sand. "Should we move them?" he asks.

"They're harmless," Jess tells him, "and they'll be gone by morning. You know they're ninety-five percent water. They just sort of leak into the beach. In English, it's called *deliquescence*."

Suddenly, the girl turns to her father and says, "Mamma was naked with Lola in the studio."

There's not a breath of breeze around them. Jess tips his head, looks at Daphne.

Daphne says to the girl, "Sweetheart, *I* was naked, not Lola."

"This isn't getting much better," Jess says.

"My towel fell," Daphne says. "It's a story for another time."

The family is quiet, tentative at the water's edge. The afternoon wind has died, and the sea is calm. It would be inviting, were it not for the bloom of jellies. The girl already has her feet in the water and seems to be charting a course through the alien masses.

"This is not my idea of paradise," Jess says. "Let's go around the point and see if Pachia Ammos is clear."

Daphne doesn't move. She looks around at the creatures on the beach, stranded between ugliness and beauty, gloriously interchangeable, all water and membrane and letting go. "Or we can find a way to love this," she says, "where we are. We find a new way."

"I don't love it," the boy says decisively. "I think they're gross."

"What about you?" she says to Jess, already loving it a little, this deliquescence.

He stands there beside her, looking not at the sand or the water but at her looking, as if trying to see what she sees.

When Daphne and the students enter the studio the next morning while Jess cleans up after coffee in the courtyard, Stefan stops short.

He says her name in a small gasp, and the others instinctively move away. Taking a step forward, Daphne looks first at the empty stand in front of them, where she has been working, and then at the floor, where the beautiful sculpture lies in three large pieces, the more delicate parts scattered in smaller fragments around them.

Daphne feels not so much loss as fear. In the absence of evidence, someone says something about the cats. But there had been no cats in the studio when they opened the door. And the marble—Daphne knew it was perfectly balanced, as a good sculpture should be.

Daphne cringes, hearing the car on the access road as Jess leaves with the kids for sailing club. Would he be so cruel? So imposing of an ego—if not his own, then hers? She cannot look at the others for fear that they might read her thoughts. They have not been unaware of the tensions between her and Jess. But as she turns, finally, to get an empty clay flower pot for gathering the smaller pieces, her eyes meet Lola's, and she knows.

When Jess gets back to the house and hears about the "accident," it's clear he believes Daphne smashed the sculpture herself. They're standing in the kitchen. "No one knows what happened. I'll tell Benny," Daphne says.

She tries not to show the emotion tightening her chest. But Jess, seeing, puts down the knife he's using to cut lemons and takes her in his arms more tenderly than he has done in a very long time. "I'm sorry, Daphne," he says. Though he must be relieved that Benny will not take credit for her work, he says, "It was an exquisite piece. I wouldn't have wished for you to . . . for this to happen. I said some ugly things. You could have just told him it wasn't his."

Daphne wouldn't have minded if Benny had taken credit for her work in the studio. And she will now take credit for what Lola has done out of jealousy or anger or to protect her from being used by Benny when she didn't need protecting. There is no reason for Daphne to defend the self she is learning to let go, against what Jess thinks she's done to preserve it. Even less reason to make Jess speculate on Lola's aggravated motives, of which she is now regretful. She has hurt Lola. That she will take credit for. And she'll probably tell Jess eventually. Maybe Jess doesn't know the half of it, but on some level, he gets it. How deep these things go. How unfixed are he and she in this life of theirs together. They will continue to surprise one another. And Daphne wants to love him better.

"I'm sorry too," she says, the cicadas at full throb in the fields around the house and in all of the absent trees. It is and isn't about her. Like the sky. Like the sea and its jellies. All of the boundaries are loosening.

Jess releases her. "But you're sculpting again," he says.

"Yes," Daphne says. She feels as brokenhearted as a planet, but also devoted to this life she has chosen. To the art of subtraction, the medium of stone.

Benny drops by in the evening, finding Daphne and Jess in the garden. He says there's been a change of plans, and he wonders if he might get a refund for the last two days since he won't be around. He's leaving that night on the ferry for Athens. Jess says no.

When Daphne explains to Benny that the sculpture is broken, he shakes his head and laughs a little. He sets his daypack down on the table in the garden and pulls from it a small marble replica of a Cycladic figure, the one known as the Flute Player. This he admits to having bought in town two days before, worried that his wife wouldn't like the piece Daphne had made. "No offense," he says.

It was just that easy.

The Intervention

The nun wants to kill the dog. The dog has a cancer on its head the size and color of a testicle, and it is growing daily. And the nun's own days are inflected with grief—grief and also something more. At meditation she is not centered in the hara, two inches below her navel. Instead, she gravitates to that canker, a crass red distorting the dog's head, or the eye of the dog that pleads with her, and that is what she gives herself up to. Not the warm, slobbering tongue she used to allow to take chunks of oily potato from her hand when she cleaned up in the refectory, but the dog's corrosive need.

    She is a Buddhist. In the Indian village of McLeod Ganj, where exiled Tibetan monasteries scale the foothills of the Himalayas alongside tourist hotels, she has sat under the teaching of the Dalai Lama. She knows well that the way to escape suffering is not to kill but rather to lose desire. All sentient life is sacred. She will find the way to inner peace through respect for it. But does a testicle glisten? She has never seen one—not that of a man. She hopes it does not.

    She is a nun, and because her abbess has forbidden her to kill the dog, she has decided to enlist the help of mercenaries. The day she hurries up the long, rickety stairway to the room where the Canadian woman stays, the little flyers for language tuition and a

Peace Corps party flutter in her wake, paying her more attention than she has attracted in a long time.

She has seen the Canadian woman around McLeod Ganj. They have spoken once. Or perhaps not spoken when, waiting for the bus to the lower village, they saw the dog, lying at the side of the road in the throes of a seizure, legs rigid, head bulged obscenely. Some Gujarati boys laughed at the dog, and a man in a pillbox hat—a Kashmiri man—tossed the butt of a cigarette at it. There was the smell of singed hair as the oily backside of the dog was kindled. The Canadian woman shouted in English at the man. She threw her own jacket over the dog. Its body had been released by its brain, but it was too exhausted to lick its wounds.

Nothing more has passed between them.

The nun knows where she is likely to find the Canadian woman, and when she knocks at the door—the evening windy and bone-chilling, a few stars punching out their code between rapid bursts of cloud—the Canadian asks her in. She tells the nun eagerly that she came to Dharamshala, to India, for enlightenment. To learn the ways of compassion. She wants to be of use. The Canadian speaks a little Tibetan, the nun a little English, and they make a plan. The nun will enlist Jampa, a nonpracticing Buddhist she knows, a one-time monk, to hold the dog. The Canadian, who is familiar with horses and has given injections before, will get the drug. Though the nun is still tormented by her abbess's prohibition and by the tumult of her own convictions, she will not be the one to kill the dog.

Jampa left the monastery when he was twenty-six and became a translator. Nearly thirty now, he is good-looking, his black hair drawn into a ponytail with streaks of silver in it. He and the nun met one summer while they sat under the Dalai Lama's teaching on mindfulness and the body. Jampa impressed her—and frightened her some—with his probing questions. She has heard that he is also good at what he does now: carrying meaning across the craggy geographies of language. Uncovering the intentions behind the words. But the way he looks at her when she asks for what she wants him to do—as if she were taking advantage of his lack of scruples—shames her. It is true that since he left the monastery, she has kept her distance from him. Not trusting what his own intentions might now be. Still, she does not think she is capable of the deed on her own. She needs the power of Jampa's ambivalence. And yes. What she believes to be his lapsed ethics.

Jampa agrees, but only reluctantly, to help her with the dog.

The nun has seen a child's testicles more than once. She remembers the seams in them like in a Parisian woman's hose, which she has also seen, in an advertisement in an outdated magazine. But she has never seen a man's. And not since her hair was shaved with her vows, the dark, straight clumps of it falling around her feet, has she found it so difficult to accept and dismiss her desire. But now the violation of dharma she has so deliberately set about has lifted the latch on other possible violations—on the small door of desire that feels more like curiosity or maybe anger. Jampa does not close the door behind her when she leaves his room. She listens for it but is aware of it open at her back.

Night of a gauzed-over half-moon, a mile outside the village. The road is deserted, the temperature falling quickly in the thin mountain air. The dog, as if by appointment, scampers sidelong to the place the Canadian and the nun hoped they would find him. The nun has pilfered some bones from the garbage behind a restaurant in the town below. No potatoes. Meat this time. Jampa will hold him. The Canadian will give him the needle.

Though the Canadian has brought a cricket bat for protection, she and the nun are both a bit afraid, out alone on the Bhagsu road at night. Children from the Tibetan orphanage have been raped by autorickshaw drivers there, and two Scandinavian women disappeared recently when they set out walking from McLeod Ganj. The Kashmiris were blamed for that, but the Kashmiris weren't the ones who drove the rickshaws. Anyway, they tell themselves the shadows watching them now are only junipers at the road's edge, the breathing they hear just wind in the cedars.

By the Canadian's watch, it's nine o'clock, and then ten after, and Jampa hasn't shown up. The dog licks, with little interest, the bones the nun has brought. Even his appetite is failing him, and he soon stands up and whimpers.

The nun pets his shabby hindquarter, tries to mollify him. Sweet mutt. They listen in the dark and hear only the groan of a truck's gears as it labors up the mountain across the valley. Five more minutes pass, and the dog gets up as if to leave. What can they do but try to administer the anesthesia themselves?

There is no place to grab the dog. He nips at the nun's hand when she puts it anywhere close to his head. She straddles him, holding him by the shoulders. She strokes his neck lovingly. Suspicious now, he tries to back out from between her legs, so she squeezes hard with her knees. She tells herself she is merely trying to comfort him, but he is not comforted. He whines miserably until, suddenly, he slumps to the ground beneath her.

The Canadian kneels beside the dog. Pulling her long hair back with one hand, she kneads the shoulder of the dog with the other, then feels around with a finger. But unlike a horse's hide, the dog's skin is obscured by thick, mangy fur. She can't find the vein. They haven't thought to bring a razor. It's also dark, and they forgot about a flashlight. "Where the fuck is Jampa?" the Canadian mutters, angry now. A mist is settling over the mountain. The sound of another motor not so far off reminds them they need to hurry. The Canadian grabs a fold of skin and fur from the region of the animal's neck and shoulder. She jabs the needle in blindly, dispenses the fluid with her thumb. But the dog stands up as if merely reproached and stumbles as he tries to bolt. "Do something!" the Canadian shouts, diving for his hindquarters. The dog is disoriented and able to run only in a tight circle to the right. The nun picks up the paddle and, blinded by a fury that wells up out of her thwarted compassion, she strikes the dog on the head. She strikes it again and again, hears the cracking of the skull.

Jampa is, at that moment, having tea with his friend Dorjee at the Peace Café in McLeod Ganj. They are talking about the poems that Jampa is trying, with only moderate success, to bring from Tibetan into English. The little white ruffled curtains are drab against the night windows, but the tea is warm and the conversation good, even when it wanders toward the mundane. Though no one has forbidden him, this is not a night when Jampa wants to kill a dog. Dorjee is saying that if he ever moves to Austria, he hopes to open a massage parlor that serves momos, but he is willing to wash dishes or care for children. Dorjee will do anything. But there are things that Jampa is not willing to do.

The nun he has stood up on her killing mission is more beautiful than Jampa will admit. Her face has a pattern of discoloration near the edge that makes him see her in mottled layers. Her eyes are the brightest green, her lower lip tucked beneath her upper lip in a way he tries not to think about. He has been acquainted with her two or three years, since she came to Dharamshala on leave from another monastery to study. For reasons Jampa doesn't know, she never went back. After he left the monastery, she rarely talked to him when he saw her at the vegetable stands or in the street. He and Dorjee are startled when she bursts into the café and demands that Jampa go with her.

Which he does. He follows her through the streets, where stick fires have been kindled in the gutters, and men squatting around them talk in low voices. She leads him to his own room. He opens the door. The walls inside are insulated with newspapers, and when he flicks on the light, he is suddenly aware of having warmed himself with atrocities and natural disasters and political scandals. On the counter, parings of the vegetables from his dinner remain. Turning on the light, he can see that there is blood on her hands. She tells him, "Take off your clothes." She is dead sober.

When, baffled, he begins by unbuttoning his shirt, she says, "Your trousers." Her eyes, dark and almost wholly occupied by the black disks of the pupils, would have told him, even without the blood, that she has killed the dog.

"Is this a rape?" he says.

She shakes her head. No. So he steps out of his pants and then, looking into her face, hesitates. She nods, and he removes his undergarments too. He stands before her like that, naked but for his shirt.

"How did you do it?" he says.

"I beat it to death with a cricket bat. I bashed its skull in."

He indicates the sink in the corner of the room. "Do you want to wash your hands?"

She doesn't move.

"And do you blame me for that?" he says.

She does not know how to tell him what she wants. When she had begun to batter it, the dog had yelped and whined. To make it stop, she had had to continue. It had begun to stagger in a circle. She wasn't sure when the dog had given up because she was still hammering its skull when out of the eventual silence, broken only by the crazy thud of the bat, she heard the Canadian pleading with her to stop.

She wants, now, to see something beautiful. If she will pay in the next life for what she has done, she wants to steal some small pleasure. The pleasure of looking. She will not spend what remains of her life imagining the private parts of a man as ulcerous knobs.

But the testicles are humble, brownish, not at all, in the end, like the dog's cancer. Deferential pouches of skin as nonchalant as bundles carried home at the end of a long day.

The Canadian came to Dharamshala to be of use—driven, perhaps, by vestiges of faith. But she has been of no more use to anyone here than she was to anyone at home. On the mission of mercy for the dog, what she made possible, or necessary, with her great heart and even greater lack of experience, bore little resemblance to an act of compassion. She'd had to pull the deranged nun off and coax her like a wary animal back to the village before either of them did the dog any more favors.

The next morning, having slept little, the Canadian revises her life's ambitions. She will most likely not ever be of use. What she seeks now is closure.

Turning out the Bhagsu road, she passes the tattoo parlor and a few last buildings that are like a grunt and a sigh as the road leaves the village. She approaches the place where she and the nun left the dog. Where, currently, some Gujarati boys she knows from the tent city below the lower village are attempting to burn it. They are the same boys who were laughing at the dog a few days ago at the bus stop. Scaring off the vultures, they have succeeded only in depilating one side and creating a stench.

When not lighting dogs, these boys beg in the upper village for "milk for the baby," which the Canadian happens to know they sell in a prearranged deal back to the store. There is no baby anymore. Their mother has gone off—nobody knows where. All the days the Canadian has worked to persuade their alcoholic father he should allow them to go to school are hanging over her now, the opposite of enlightenment. Two weeks ago, a tourist gave the smartest of the boys five thousand rupees. Now the boys are too valuable for the father to spare.

She is angry with them for doing so well what she wants them not to do at all. She is angry that they are friendly when they want things from her. Seeing their delight in the wreckage they've happened upon, the hash of the dog's brain an open story for which they will fashion their own ending, she hates them a little.

The lie she finds herself telling them surprises even her, though she believes they have it coming. "Your momma," she says, "is looking for you in McLeod Ganj."

They drop their sticks, and the one holding the lighter, the most charismatic one, the sweetest little brown-faced work-you-like-a-fucker con man of all, stands and walks over to her. Scrutinizing her expression, he challenges her. "Say that again." If nothing else, they believe she is honest. Reliable in a way that no one else in their lives, current or past, has been.

There is satisfaction in the power she feels as they shrug their bony shoulders and consider this reversal in their fortunes. Satisfaction that's like nothing she has felt since she arrived in this place.

She watches their gangly outlines disappear. Then she slumps against a juniper a few yards back from the road to witness, at the approach of each autorickshaw or taxi, the only resurrection she still believes possible. Vultures carrying pink shreds of meat skyward.

And what, Jampa wonders, is he to the nun, that she would think to use him as a proxy for her indiscretions? The night before, had she tried to punish him for having let her down? For not having turned up at the appointed time?

Naked, he had stood in front of her, watching her regard him. Perhaps she had wanted to *be* punished. Or to be loved. Jampa didn't think he loved her. Nor did he love being used by her. Either way, in spite of himself, under her gaze he was aroused.

He went to her and brusquely removed first the pilled acrylic sweater and then her robe. Was this what she wanted?

The dusty hiking boots on her small feet were knotted, so he left them. He laid her on the bed and straddled her, aligning his body with hers. Because she did not speak, he could not know what she was thinking. Her mouth did not touch him, but he thrust roughly into the small opening of her.

Afterward, she asked him to turn out the light before she stood up and, like someone used to waking in the smallest hours, dressed herself in the dark. Fearful in the silence that could mean anything, or nothing, he said to her, "Now see what you have done."

Vertigo

Marvin didn't just wake up one day and realize history was repeating itself. It happened gradually, the same way his hairline receded or he could no longer say on medical forms that he would describe himself as healthy. And was *he* the one who had insisted on the black refrigerator that Cynthia said made the kitchen look outdated? Would the stainless steel one have confirmed their place in the present?

Either way, Marvin feels most sure of himself when he is standing in the kitchen, frying eggs for Cynthia after the pancakes he's made for himself. The cat, which he calls Bunion and Cynthia calls Juniper, rubs against his leg.

Sometimes, though, when he is mowing the lawn or sitting outside with his in-laws, he has the distinct impression that they are all sinking. Into the little bog that forms there when it rains hard on the tail end of a hurricane down the coast. They'll be sitting and talking about nothing in particular, and he'll begin to see them all with blackened limbs—though still with red hair because they're Scots-Irish. Like the bog people he saw at the museum in Chicago last fall because Cynthia had thought the exhibit sounded fascinating. And a little spooky. The people were shriveled and not all that well preserved—at least not how he had expected. They were victims of violence, mostly.

As the light fades and the sun disappears behind the arborvitae separating their yard from the neighbors' and he feels himself and his company sinking, he moves his chair closer to the fire they've laid in the fire ring. He bends down and pulls up his socks. No one else notices. Cynthia seems fine, but he's a little spooked.

———

Mostly, Marvin has stopped watching the news because it's depressing. He used to watch Peter Jennings after long days at the car dealership. He feels a warm glow even now thinking of Jennings' face. The integrity of it. Anymore, you just couldn't tell really. Cynthia says, "Oh yes, white men are awfully comforting, aren't they?" It's not that though. You used to be able to watch the news and believe what it told you. How was anyone supposed to know what was happening these days?

Tonight, for instance, they're talking about this Syrian refugee on a Greek island. Do you believe what they said yesterday (he was a poor man in need of asylum) or what they're saying today (ISIS beheader)? And if he is a member of ISIS, does it follow that, as one commentator suggests, many of the other Syrian refugees are also ISIS? Who knows? They're moving on to the new virus that has swept some province in China and now has shown up in the US. How dangerous is it? Nothing to worry about, or a twenty-first-century plague?

Marvin says aloud, "So which news is supposed to be fake? Not Fox, right?" That's what he's been watching. But Cynthia must have drifted out somewhere between the threat of terrorism and the threat of pandemic. "Cynthia," he says gently. Sometimes he leaves her there on the couch because she has a hard time getting back to sleep if she moves. She looks different when she falls asleep by accident. The weariness goes out of her face in a way it never does with deliberate sleep. "Cynthia, don't you want to come to bed?"

Marvin is glad they have found something to give their lives meaning in the midst of so much badness, and the men in the church breakfast group had said they liked Fox News. Marvin and Cynthia had begun going to church just about a year before, when some friends invited them. Marvin had reached a point of burnout on a personal level. At the Ford dealership, each time he made a sale, he could think only of the melancholy that would set in for the buyers once the new-car smell wore off. Every day reminded him how temporary happiness was. How shifty. Not that he was really doing anything wrong, but what he was selling people—material happiness for as high a price as they would pay—never felt quite right either. It paid the bills, which was what it seemed his life had come to.

So it was Marvin who'd really wanted to keep going to church once they'd visited. He'd felt at least like he was getting his bearings again. Cynthia liked the social aspects of it well enough. She'd been raised in the church, so it was easy for her to fall back into the current, saying creeds with her fingers crossed as necessary.

"All the networks are controlled by a plot to topple Trump," Marvin's neighbor, Greg, says over the rhodies one day when they are both out watering because of an unseasonable drought. Marvin doesn't know what to say. "You better believe it," Greg says. He goes to the same church Marvin and Cynthia do. Greg says the networks hate Christians. Well, real Christians, anyway. Except for Fox News, maybe. He waves the fan of water back and forth over the grass seed he has planted in spite of the weather. In fact, neither of them is supposed to be watering at the moment on account of the drought. But if there's one thing they agree on, it's personal freedom. And that means nobody saying when and how much they can turn on the hose. They don't agree on the gun issue. Greg exercises his right to bear arms. Marvin thinks there should be more limits. He notices that Greg always has his hose nozzle set to its most forceful fire.

Marvin has been told his red hair, like his baldness, is due to a recessive gene. He also understands from his student days that a recessive gene can make things go haywire. Cause a disease, for example, if it is a mutation and it meets up with the right partner. Or, more accurately, the wrong partner. Case in point, his cousin's cystic fibrosis.

So a few days later, when he is down at Shop 'n Save and he begins to feel that slippage happening again, he has to wonder if it's some weird genetic thing. Or if there's been some kind of invasion of his mind. He's there in the meat section when labels he's never before paid attention to begin to catch his eye. Gluten-free turkey breast at the deli counter! He thought gluten was a bread thing. He wasn't sure what was supposed to be wrong with it (though Cynthia knew), but did this mean he'd been eating glutinated turkey? He moves along the aisle to steaks, which are marked "No Dyes." When he flees to the produce aisle, he picks up an orange certified to be grown without pesticides and finished without irradiation.

He's never knowingly bought a dyed steak or an irradiated orange. How can he believe what he sees today when he was so wrong in yesterday's assumptions?

Are the fluorescent lights flickering? He picks up a package of two turkey drumsticks and sniffs it, even though it is covered in plastic wrap. Two women, who are also handling the drumsticks, are wearing cloth masks that cover their mouths and noses. What the hell? Are they afraid of contamination? Joining this band of label-readers, the skeptics, the wary scavengers, he feels like a throwback to days of yore. When was yore? He feels things going medieval on him. There's a Dark Ages gloom, and now, yes, the fluorescent lights go out. It's been hot, and there are gray-outs. But these people around him—they're not locals. Who are they? He squeezes his eyes shut and opens them again. There's a woman wearing a doeskin jacket pounding on the butcher's cooler door. A terrible stench of rotting meat fills his olfactories, and he needs to get out of the store. He's pretty sure he sees a couple of rats scurry past his feet down by the breakfast sausages.

Marvin is loyal. He has a good heart. But by the time he gets home, his heart is filled with mistrust. Gone is the spirit of loving-kindness with which he had started the day, with which he broke and fried two eggs—eggs he never dreamed were laid by a hormonal chicken. He doesn't like anyone lying to him.

Here's the thing about Cynthia, though. She adapts. When everyone started doing Zumba, Cynthia got rid of her stepping block for aerobics and joined up. Cynthia stopped eating gluten because she read that it would help her not get Alzheimer's. She had gone from butter to margarine, back to butter, and then on to coconut oil. She'd been a carnivore, an omnivore, a pescatarian, and a Presbyterian before becoming a gluten-free Evangelical. She'd been a Democrat, an unaffiliated voter, and a Girl Scout leader.

Now, Marvin has apparently stimulated further adaptations. When he gets home that evening, Cynthia has dinner piping hot on the table. She prays that God will drain the swamp and bless their food and their conversation. When she says that, "drain the swamp," Marvin remembers his twilit vision of a couple of days before. He tries not to imagine Cynthia becoming a bog person, or himself either. She bites into a gluten-free dinner roll she made from the *Artisanal Breads Adapted for Gluten-Free Living* book. Why does she think their conversation needs blessing?

Cynthia doesn't give him much time to puzzle over that. "Marvin," she says, setting the partially eaten roll on her plate decisively, "you're not going to like what I have to tell you."

"OK..." he says, still holding his fork on the way to his mouth. He hasn't told her what happened at the store, or what's been happening to him at all lately, so he is almost a little relieved to know she has something too.

"It's about Lars."

"Lars?"

"The children's choir director. It's about him and me."

"What do you mean?" The relief he felt drains away. "You and Lars?" He puts down the fork. "How long?"

"A few months."

Why would it matter how long? Is it a question of how much of his and Cynthia's history together he'll need to revise in his personal account?

Marvin gazes out the window, where the deer are devouring the chokeberry bush, one leafy twig at a time. He has a rival. His rival is more appealing to the female who is his wife. Is showier and more commanding. More aggressive. Has a larger rack, perhaps. "And is it still going on?" he says.

"Not really."

That's one she learned from her father. When they would cross from the US to Canada on vacation and the border agents asked had they purchased anything and were they carrying any firearms, her father always said, "No, not really." Cynthia had thought that was funny every time she told the story.

Even though Cynthia isn't *really* carrying firearms, she apparently crossed a border five months ago that Marvin didn't even know they were headed for.

That night, Marvin turns on the news, but not only Fox. He wonders what else he's been missing. Because he wants to know the truth. He does. He's just not sure about who he's chosen as its messenger. Or maybe he's trying to win Cynthia back—suspecting she only conceded to watching Fox because he wanted it and she was getting her satisfaction elsewhere. Or maybe the children's choir director watched it too. Cynthia says, "I'm sorry, Marvin, really I am. I know you're going to need time. We'll talk when you've had a chance to process this."

What Cynthia seems to think is that Marvin is going to adapt.

Fox is giving its airtime to the president again, who offers assurances that America is safe from the virus. One commentator suggests it's a hoax, meant to frighten people. Another suggests it is real and is biological warfare on the part of the Chinese. Marvin changes the channel, throwing his consciousness into the news on whatever channel is not Fox. The other networks are taking more seriously the potential of the virus to become a pandemic. They're saying it has spread to Italy, and now even California, on a cruise ship.

The reporters are talking about various kinds of disinformation they claim the president has been tweeting. They're saying he is pulling out of the Paris climate accords. Or the Paris Peace Accords. Wait, no. It's his secret meetings with the Russians. Or the North Vietnamese. Or the Russians. Uh-oh. He's slipping. And as Marvin is sitting there, the station goes to static. Off the air. It's like something that used to happen when he was little and they stayed up too late watching.

A banner flashes across the screen, saying that viewers should turn to Channel 11 for the official news. The fake news channels have, apparently, been shut down. "Cynthia, this is bad," he says, but she has already drifted off. He flips from channel to channel, finding no news stations, but ads for the politburo instead. They're building a wall. At first, he's sure it's at the Rio Grande, to stop the Mexicans coming over, but then he sees they're in Berlin. There are nationalistic photos of Unter den Linden, the street in Communist East Berlin with its neoclassical museums. What he thinks is Fox, the official channel now, is telling everyone to stay home. The wall went up in the night and no one can leave, but the news says it's an *antifascist protection wall*.

Cynthia has taken on the look of an exhausted East German hausfrau, bedraggled even though she has fallen asleep by mistake. Burning the candle at both ends. He finds himself wondering if the choir director is Stasi, threatening her if she doesn't cooperate. The ads on TV have the distinct flavor of propaganda. Marvin staggers into the kitchen to get an orange, but the fruit basket is full of dried biscuits. And when the news turns to the nation's leader, it's an old, white guy, but they're calling him Erich Honecker. He's telling them to trust only what they hear from the government through the government news outlet. When Marvin smashes the remote down on the coffee table, the back drops off and a funny little wire falls out. He takes Cynthia by the arms and shakes her awake.

"Was machst du?" she says.

He puts a finger to his lips to silence her, indicating the dismantled remote. Then he goes to the front door, opens it, and looks out onto the street. Down near the Hackenbergs' place, at the end of the block, a makeshift guard platform has gone up. He can see the Funkturm too, in the distance. The iconic East German radio tower. Stranger still, he knows what it is. How long have they been lied to?

At the same time that he is there, living this nightmare in the present, he also knows what comes after: the decades of oppression and the controlled flow of information to the public. The enforced isolation. The rotten system of surveillance. The power grabs at the top. The corruption of ideals into a new authoritarianism. He knows. And there, atop the guard platform is his neighbor, Greg, with a military rifle and a huge spotlight that lands right in his face.

"What's going on?" Marvin shouts to Greg.

"Pretty nifty, huh? No gray area anymore," Greg says, shining the searchlight along the makeshift wall and then back at Marvin. "You know which side you're on."

But Marvin doesn't know, really. In the next few weeks, the slippage gets worse. He complains to Cynthia of a kind of vertigo but doesn't go into detail. The pandemic gets worse too. Or else it doesn't. It depends on who you ask. They are, at any rate, calling it a pandemic now, and it worries Marvin, but however bad it is in some places—cruise ships and maybe Brooklyn—it hasn't made its way to their town. And some people are still saying it's a hoax.

At church the next Sunday, the pastor's message, refusing to be sidetracked by the "so-called pandemic," is about the threat of Islam to the Christian world, about the way Christianity is being targeted by the broadband humanists under the guise of diversity. After communion, the children's choir gets up to sing, and Marvin feels a little faint—a little nauseous. They're singing a medley of songs with gory themes. *What can make me whole again? Nothing but the blood of Jesus.* The grape juice he has swallowed along with the fleshy bread churns in his gut, and the singing makes him feel a little like a cannibal, having celebrated human sacrifice. Then they're on to *the armor of salvation* and *the weapon of His love*, and Marvin stands and begins to push his way past several kneeling parties to go to the men's room. But they're singing *Deep inside this armor, the warrior is a child*, and he can't get by because the worshippers are growing enthused, and a cry rises up from the congregation.

People are on their feet now. The choir director, already exposed to Marvin as a fraud, is waving a baton high in the air. He has the look of a man who believes the world should be his—whatever he wants of it. Marvin feels the press of the crowd; they're climbing over the pews and pushing toward the narthex, where they will leave the church, inspired by the voices of heavily indoctrinated youth.

Marvin looks for Cynthia amid the Jesus banners. The women are retreating to the church basement to make bone broth or card ewes' wool for sweaters and to pray for the safety of the men and the children going off to kill the infidel. Marvin runs against the current toward the basement steps, trying to make it to the Wesley Room, but he is knocked down and he remembers battling the feet and dark-socked ankles of zealots before the lay leader lands with a knee on his skull and he loses consciousness.

In the car on the way home from the hospital, Cynthia refuses to talk about what happened, though he has battle scars to prove it—a black eye, a concussion, an aura of defeat. "You're losing perspective, Marvin," is all she can say. She claims not to have seen what went on, and now he's pretty sure she wasn't in the Wesley Room at all with the females of the species. In the chaos of the moment, she was almost certainly in the closet of the choir room with Lars. He can't believe she has *really* fallen for that self-righteous creep. Whatever Marvin is losing, it definitely isn't perspective.

"You had a fall. You hit your head. It must have been the vertigo thing."

"I'm not going there anymore," he tells her.

"To church? Who's making you go?" Cynthia says, throwing her hands up in exasperation. "Have I ever made you go?"

"You seem to need a chaperone, and I've participated willingly in ritualized cannibalism for well over a year, but I draw the line at holy war."

"Jesus, Marvin. Your jealousy doesn't warrant a war on Christendom. I'm glad you're drawing the line somewhere."

Marvin has to wonder if it's all of them slipping or really just him. He knows that what's happening isn't because of what Cynthia has told him, since it started before that. Still, he admits he is suspicious almost all of the time now, and the whole business has gotten worse since he found out about Cynthia and Lars. In spite of her collusion in the East Germany scene, Cynthia never talks about what's happening. He thinks she really doesn't see it. Besides, the news channels are all there the next time he goes to look, which comes as a huge relief, because he's thinking now that even if you say something enough times and plant enough mistrust of the opposition that people will believe you, as the president has claimed, this doesn't make it true. So he watches a different channel each night. Certain themes emerge: disinformation campaigns exposed, secret meetings, firings, investigations shut down, scapegoats, more firings, lies.

Marvin and Cynthia have a dinner party that turns into the fall of Rome. They crawl to their beds stuffed and drunk, still in their clothes and tempted by other people's spouses' prophetic views on the end times. By the time they get there, Marvin feels positively primordial. He watches Cynthia get back out of bed in the dark, soon after they have gotten in, and lumber into the bathroom. Her feet thump the floorboards, and then he hears her sigh as she sits down and pees. Not a tinkle but a steady, obstinate stream, and this he finds comforting, though it is at the same time a sound he does not love. It is an ancient sound, older than the plague. As old as hominids living on hard surfaces. Peeing in caves. Peeing on dead leaves. Peeing on stone as smooth as porcelain. Who are they and how can he love her now?

Their little civilization will fall as so many have fallen before. Their marriage has failed to perpetuate the species. And will fail, period. Even without their help, the species might do itself in.

For a moment, he feels such tenderness, or compassion, maybe, that when she returns, he reaches across the bed to touch her face. But she is either sleeping already or pretending to sleep in her smooth, womanly skin—skin she has restored with expensive products in the bathroom before coming to bed. Skin that does not want to be touched. Or not by him.

The dinner party had been Cynthia's idea. She had thought it would help to be surrounded by people who cared about them and who would be a reality check for Marvin. The disaster came into clear focus when Marvin stumbled into an argument (one Cynthia later claimed he had instigated) over whether or not the spread of the virus, which had begun to gain ground in the US, could be contained. Cynthia's friend from work—her boss, actually—said it was unavoidable. Like climate change, it was part of the natural cycle. The strong would survive.

"And the less strong? The old people? The fat people? The Mexicans?"

"You called it."

Marvin said he felt bad for those people—people who might die if somebody didn't try to stop it.

"You do that and you reduce us to the lowest common denominator. Think about the gene pool," the boss said.

Marvin chugged his whiskey and Coke. Pouring another, he said, "Now you're really talking like a Nazi." Admittedly, he had taken it too far.

Afterward, he retreated to the back deck to watch the gangly, white neighbor boys—Greg's teenage sons—play basketball under a utility light by the garage next door. They played against two Mexican-looking guys, who were shorter but clearly more agile, and fiercer. Probably smarter too. One of the Latinos went for a layup. Game point. The white guys high-fived the other two, who picked up their T-shirts from the hedge where they'd thrown them and walked off down the driveway.

In the vertiginous days after the party, the term "news anchor" takes on new meaning for Marvin. Each time he feels himself drifting, he grabs the remote and turns on the news. He moves deliberately from one channel to the next, feeling how the gravity of events and the reporting from different sources, different points of view, grounds him. He starts watching public television, which isn't controlled by advertising interests.

Going to the carnival is Marvin's idea. He invites Cynthia, as if he needed to do that formally. As if they were merely dating. Cynthia says yes, though he knows she might rather stay home alone. But if history really is repeating itself, and if they are all slipping backward in time, he'd like to be strapped in for the ride—and yes, he would like to have Cynthia by his side. She hasn't asked for his forgiveness, which incidentally, he is mostly prepared to give, but not while she is only "not really" sleeping with the Crusader.

The carnival does not disappoint. Some people are wearing masks, but most are not. Calliope music fills the early-evening air, which smells of sweetness and hot grease from the food trucks. The dogwood trees are in blossom, and the high school students on parade—girls arm in arm, three across; boys in nervous packs, their pants riding low on their hips, their heads turning as the girls pass. Their attentions will not be acknowledged until later, when one girl will say to the other that she saw one of the guys looking at her friend. Does she want to go over to the Tilt-A-Whirl? That's the direction the guys are headed. Each gesture is ancient—each coupling under the grandstand or behind the restrooms almost older than time, though the young people don't understand this yet.

Cynthia loves the rides that turn her upside down and spin her abruptly in more dimensions than she thought possible. She forgoes these on Marvin's account—because of his vertigo. They both know this is her kindness to him: tonight, she won't try to persuade. He attempts the Italian swings willingly but steps off feeling more like a squid than something with a backbone. It's no wonder that someone like Cynthia has helped humanity to thrive, in spite of people like himself. He encourages her to go ride the Salt and Pepper Shaker while he sits down to recover. Cynthia grins and hurries off.

Marvin glances at his watch. It's nearly six. They'll miss the news. He has been sitting for just a few minutes, waiting for the green feeling to subside, when he notices, directly opposite the bench, the opening to a Ripley's Believe It or Not! House of Oddities. He's always wondered about such things—were they real? He is pretty sure freak shows are against the law these days. But the Human Pincushion? At least that would be a voluntary thing, as opposed to a birth defect making somebody a spectacle.

Inside the doorway, he is shunted down a makeshift corridor in low light. The first display, on the left, features malformed fetuses preserved in canning jars. It's difficult to tell whether they are human or not, though the sign claims they are all spontaneously aborted specimens of the human race. Some have tiny extra limbs, extra heads, arms that appear to grow out of heads. Some are knitted together in a pair. He knows he is supposed to feel aversion. Or sick fascination. But what he feels is a bit of an ache in his chest for what he shares with these creatures fixed in their deformities. Each body manifests some mutation, maybe some recessive quality asserted before birth. It strikes Marvin, now, as a kind of suppressed memory. Of accidents, or ancestors. He and Cynthia have talked about being born again. But he suspects, now, that they have not been. All that they were born with the first time is still there, and they will have to live with it.

He moves along, his shoes sticking to the plywood boardwalk where people have spilled soft drinks and popcorn and dropped space-age ice cream pellets. The genius Albert Einstein appears to be made entirely of toast. Marvin is aware that he both believes and does not believe the illusion.

Before he gets to the Pincushion Man, he passes a series of photographs. There is a "Cyclops goat." One big eye with a rectangular pupil, centered on its forehead, stares directly at him. An "authentic" cannibal poses frankly, without any other hint of savagery, behind four neat human skulls displayed on a table. Like some of the others photographed, the man looks directly at the viewer. There's a "vampire woman" with long, fang-like canines, her body covered in tattoos. That one looks as though it might have been Photoshopped, like the ones that made Michelle Obama look like a man. How willingly he has sometimes been deluded! When he reaches the Wolf Girl with her caveman-heavy eyebrows and facial hair, her knowing eyes seem intent on something just off to the side of him.

It's strange to be there in the House of Oddities at news hour. He's almost salivating for the ever-changing cycle of stories that will define the moment and him in it. But compared to where he is right now, that all seems a mere fetish. Each of the displays that mark his progress along the path constructed for him takes him further into the gene pool from which he has emerged and into all of the possibilities that are buried in him.

Arrows announcing the Pincushion Man appear every few yards, in case people are about to give up on ever reaching the live exhibit because someone in their party has to go to the bathroom or they're just losing interest altogether. But Marvin is deeper in than he ever wanted to be. He is full of memories, genetic and ancestral. Though he doesn't know how, exactly, he is complicit in all of this humanity. And being caught up in it feels true and enduring. The deeper he goes, the farther he feels from the exit and the possibility of emerging back into the gaiety of the fair. The Asbestos Man holds a burning match to his own jaw and doesn't flinch. Marvin thinks suddenly of Cynthia and, starting with a jolt as if he himself had felt the flame, he hurries along, past the rest of the displays and the Pincushion Man himself to the nondescript door at the end of the exhibit, through which he bursts.

Cynthia is sitting in his place on the bench, waiting. "What happened to you?" she says.

He wonders if it shows—where he has been and what it has done to him. "Am I still green?" he says. "I was just in there among the freaks and the throwbacks." He feels, immediately, the sting in his misrepresentation. We lie to each other. We do, and for lots of reasons.

Cynthia says, "I had no idea where you were."

Sometimes, though, we don't lie.

She had zipped his cell phone into her purse when they rode the Italian swings so she couldn't call. But she looks frightened now, as if, perhaps, she thinks she really has lost him, not having meant to.

"Sorry," he says. "I thought I'd just duck in for a minute, but it seemed like I was in there forever. You couldn't turn around. Look at all of these people, though."

Taking in the wild mix of the crowd, it seems to Marvin that he hasn't come out of the exhibit at all. There are really obese people and anorexics, and there are amputees and people in love and people who have lost their hair from chemo. And some of those are the people in love. There are little people and girls with wine-colored birthmarks, and there are people with eyes of two different colors. There are geniuses eating french fries—actual geniuses now made of french fries. A very heavy man who can't seem to breathe is being carried off the midway by masked EMTs toward a waiting ambulance.

As they head for the car, Marvin feels the wild world of the carnival with all of its creatures and illusions being swallowed up in an even larger world—his moment in history swallowed by the centuries and the millennia. For the first time, he welcomes the feeling.

The generators that keep the rides turning celebrate everything cyclical. They whirl people through space in tiny erratic bursts or sweep them in orderly rotations—creatures who believe or don't believe in their evolution as progress. Adrenaline recalls the animal thrills and fears and gives way afterward to the comfort of pairings or of the pack moving through the dark parking lot.

On an impulse, at the edge of the park, Marvin pulls Cynthia into an open capsule of the Ferris wheel, and the girl on duty fastens the bar across in front of them. He wonders if the girl can see how ancient he is—and if he is visibly more ancient than Cynthia. They rise and begin their circuit of the night sky.

Each time they return to the low point, they are just a little different than they were before. A little older. By turns closer to one another or more distant. More grounded or less. It is all in the realm of normal for the human experience. On the way up, they are moving backward. Then they advance down the night sky, in their seats among the hundred-year-old trees. The night is druid. They are pilgrims come from afar. It is unbelievably beautiful.

The Girl Who Loved Boyan Slat

> We're driving the largest cleanup in history. . . . We let the plastic come to us, using the ocean currents [to] our advantage.
> —BOYAN SLAT

Dear Boyan Slat,

Honestly, I thought it was beautiful how after the rain drenched everything, the creeks rummaged through the holler, coaxing out all the plastic milk jugs and Clorox bottles and grocery bags. Afterward, they hung in the trees at the waterline, like memories of days in people's lives—days that would otherwise have been lost in the murky depths of time.

Listen to me. *The murky depths of time.*

Maybe this has something to do with my being born in a town that was flooded over when they built the dam. We don't live there anymore, obviously. We moved to Rowan County when I was seven. But being born in a submerged town is something like being born with a caul, as far as I can tell. You see things through a glass, darkly. Though a caul is supposed to be lucky, and Mr. Slat, I'm about as unlucky as a cake in the rain. Referring to a song my father loved in the version by the awful and ancient Ray Conniff Singers. And that brings me to the Tupperware cake storage container my mother purchased when their love failed. My first experience of plastic as grace. Salvation. I shouldn't be leading with this. It certainly isn't my best foot forward in a letter to a guy who famously wants to clean up the world's overabundance of ocean-bound plastic. It's an honest foot though.

Also, there was the plastic glow-in-the-dark cross I kept in a shoebox in the closet after a week at Vacation Bible School. All of this in a family that started out believing in wooden toys and strictly cotton underpants.

Are you surprised that I'm writing all the way from America? I'm sending it in an actual letter in hopes you won't ignore it as shitposting. And that's a maybe. Maybe I'm sending it.

I've gotten past the religious stuff—nothing a summer of preachy work in the Appalachian hollers wouldn't cure me of. It was supposed to be a soul-winning thing—sharing the gospel with the underprivileged back in Perry County—but instead it was a graphic illustration that what seemed true for one little body just really had nothing to do with lots of other people, a Cinderella shoebox cross that didn't fit. People there had nothing and saw lots of bad shit happen—shit I really hadn't taken into account—and even had their own ideas about happiness and beauty. But the plastic endured, as well you know it does! And still with a surreptitious glow that tells me I haven't seen the end of it.

Dear Boyan Slat,

Today's letter is mostly a confession. Back from my morning run, I'm sitting out under the sweet gum tree in the yard of our house, and it's been two days since Aldo Leopold died. We buried him in a box and—don't ask me why—put him in a plastic bag inside. More hygienic, I guess. Also, there's a sweat bee on my arm.

(Aldo was a cat, by the way.) I'm eating yogurt to make myself feel better, the blended kind that comes in plastic mini cups. I've eaten four of the six in the pack—and with a plastic spoon. I'd ask if you thought less of me, but I know you don't think of me at all, or didn't, at least, until you maybe got my last letter, and maybe read it. I know you're a busy person.

Sitting here, I'm surrounded by creeping Charlie and weedy violets that have taken over the lawn. In the house, there's a three-layer Lady Baltimore cake in my mother's Tupperware container. She made it as consolation for Aldo's passing. In conclusion, death is the mother of plastic. But so is infidelity, I guess.

It was after my father left that my mother and I converted: a plastic slide in the yard, plastic straws in plastic orange-juice bottles and, for my birthday, balloons made of Mylar (isn't that plastic too?) spelling out the happiness she wished for me—the very happiness they had destroyed. I suppose you could say I am, somehow, though not profoundly, unhappy.

I'm not asking for absolution. I now believe that we live with the consequences of our actions. The same way my mother had to live with the red hair she got out of a bottle, even though it made her look like a failed teenager or the last stand of a dying coral reef. I think she hated it too, but she wore it first as an act of defiance, since my father had loved her natural dirty blonde, and later as proof that she knew what she was doing. Why are psychologists always the last to see what's going on in their own heads? I should talk though.

I'm nineteen and working part time at the Piggly Wiggly, still living at home with my mother. In my own defense, I'm thinking about community college next year. Or something. Somebody at the high school saw me out running the other day, and now they've asked me to coach the girls track team. LOL. My only excuse not to is that I'm completely unqualified.

All of this to say I imagine you somewhere out in the middle of the ocean with your team, waiting for the rain to wash these little blueberry Dannons down the gully and into the river and across half a continent to your magnificent filtration net. Maybe you would know me then—a loser with modest aspirations to change.

Dear Boyan (OK if I call you Boyan?),

I guess my mother and I were only looking for eternal life. Or, short of that, extended expiration dates. I sucked air through a plastic snorkel the first time I went underwater at the dam at Buckhorn Lake, and I wore plastic goggles when I swam with my cousins at Beaufort, South Carolina. I can't deny that plastic is the comfort of my generation—its puffy constellations of play equipment, the promise of health in bottled water, the handy food storage bags full of Goldfish or Cheerios we grew up on, the makeup compacts that were the foundation of our first loves. Even the Lycra in my leggings. Plastic is newness and fun. It's freshness and flexibility. Radical persistence. Dashboards and bird feeders and cafeteria trays and sleds. Sunglasses and floaties. Now I feel a little like an addict, looking to be free of the necessary substance.

Mr. Slat (in case I've offended):

I don't get far without it. I'm frantic in the kitchen, waving a lettuce leaf. Or at Piggly Wiggly, I get dirty looks from my fellow cashiers when my radishes dribble down the belt, making mud with the soil from loose mushrooms. And that's just me trying to put together a simple salad for my mom and myself without causing the demise of the planet.

But this isn't about me at all. Admittedly, I am a person who used to love dumps and junkyards. To see so much that was cast off and broken—the torn vinyl upholstery of the seats of old station wagons. All that evidence of human hopes gone bust. It gave me the feeling of nothing left to lose.

No, this is about how I imagine you, drifting over the Great Pacific Garbage Patch, at just twenty or twenty-two having thrown over your education to try to fix the thing you hated about the world. And beneath you, that mass of plastic belches and churns, eighty-seven tons of it like a melting pot of the world's efficiency and immediate gratification. It's this vision of you that is making me love the possibilities of my new life as a born-again former plastics queen.

So how did you come to believe you could do shit on such an enormous scale while I'm here laying plastic geraniums on the grave of my ideals? I don't want this to come out wrong, but it seems so big, what you're up to, it's almost spiritual. The only other things I can think of that big are nuclear disasters, Islam, and Christianity.

And, to continue in the vein of honesty, I'm eaten up with disgust at my failures. Also, I'm seeing someone. He's working toward management at a company in Louisville that makes hangers for lingerie, etc. Do those things get recycled at all? If I leave them at the store, does that make me an activist?

I mean, we're not serious, him and me. Or not committed in the ultimate sense. He's a good person, really. And look who's talking! I use those little eyedrop vials about ten times a day—more on a bad day—and dental picks once in the morning and once before bed. It all seemed fine until I read about you in *National Geographic* and also started thinking about sea turtles. I didn't feel lost until then. Do you think I'm still looking for a savior? Please don't answer.

Dear Boyan,

I'm leaving him, though no, we weren't living together. I put my belongings in a cloth bag meant for laundry. I've been brushing my teeth with coconut oil and charcoal on a bamboo stick, and I'm coming your way. I've stopped wearing lingerie on account of how it's displayed. So my boobs are chafing against my shirt, and my tush is on the loose. I'm only two miles from home at present. Don't look for me any time soon. I'm at the first station of that plastic cross, which in this case is the Piggly Wiggly on State Route 189—the one where I work.

As you probably know, the impeachment hearings are on the horizon here in America—one more reminder we shouldn't put our faith in men. And still, based off the seductive dream of you on the floating island of refuse, looking like Lord of the Rings with your Bilbo Baggins face and your honest eyes, I wonder if maybe I still haven't learned.

I haven't exactly planned things out for the Piggly Wiggly "action," so I just kind of approach people at the entrance, saying things like, "Hey, forget your reusable bag?" or "Did you see they found a whale with two hundred pounds of plastic in its stomach?" Most people say they didn't. "Reusable bags save the planet. Where are yours?" When I get tired of the dirty looks and the apologetic looks and tired of feeling like the Book of Jonah there in the parking lot, I go inside and ask to talk to my manager. I ask him to donate reusable bags, which I will be happy to hand out. Get this, Boyan: He says, "Milly, the plastic ones *are* reusable. People use them for cat litter and dog poop." (I don't help him by adding "or even burying pets.") He says people won't use special bags just because you give them away. The worst part was I couldn't argue with him. So I just left. Tail between my proverbial legs. I'm sure you would have known what to say to that, but I sure as hell did not.

Boyan, the distance between you and me is the distance between the fire alarm (which merely goes off) and the guy with the hose. The distance between the tail of the dog and genius. It's like I'm still hungover—ready to move on but with a monster headache and a thirst only a Coke would quench. I'm dying for a Coke, but I can't buy one because they only come in plastic bottles here. Where I live—and maybe you too—the world is still bingeing, but I'm the morning after.

My father, before he left, said he hoped my stubbornness would be useful one day. He was an interesting person, though not to my mother of Tupperware fame. He was the one who named our cat Aldo Leopold and, in addition to liking the ancient, sappy Ray Conniff Singers and "MacArthur Park," he thought a lot about trees and lakes. He never liked the lakes of the South—lakes formed by dams. Lakes where people drank a lot on pontoon boats and went frogging at night with searchlights. He preferred ones cut by glaciers and surrounded by birch trees and smelling of pine. Those were the lakes he'd known in his childhood up north. *For you I pine. For you I balsam.* I think he wrote that to my mother once when they were young. That was his thing. He was all about wood. Whereas I—well, no need to recap.

Because I'm not ready to go home yet, after my lame action at Piggly Wiggly, I get on the Trailways bus that happens to be parked out near the highway and cop a ticket to Louisville. It's no secret that it's hard to be an activist in your home town. Not that I am one.

So I'm sitting in the front seat, where I'll have the biggest chance of flying through the windshield if we're in a head-on with a tractor trailer, and I lean back and close my eyes and I picture your face. I picture your hands on the day's haul of plastics like a ghastly creature up from the deep. And I'm starting to see it's your optimism I'm a little in love with. Your lack of respect for the magnitude of the disaster. I mean, who, in God's holy name, believes he can clean up the planet—at least the oceans? Personally, I don't know the difference between eighty-seven tons of plastic and eighty-seven thousand tons. What I do know is that your face looks innocent, and your journey is epic.

Oh no. So it turns out there's a little engine fire toward the back of the bus, and we all pile out onto the shoulder of the highway and have to hike to the next town, a mile down the road. They can't tell us when they'll have a replacement bus, but it will be at least two hours, because that's how far we are from Louisville. I'm also remembering that I'm supposed to work in the morning.

At the minimart / diner / gas station, I'm handling the pro-life books and the antlered refrigerator magnets nearest the side window when this guy who's been sitting in a booth with his buddies gets up and walks over and asks do I need help. I'm not sure how he means, but then again, it doesn't matter. The answer is no.

"Good deal," he says. "Righty-O." He, too, begins to seem very interested in the magnets. "How about a ride?" he says. "It's a lot faster in my rig than on the bus. Especially the one that's broken down. Where you headed?"

"The Great Pacific Garbage Patch," I tell him. I may as well be headed there as to Louisville, which was just a whim anyhow.

"Is that over near Paducah?"

I laugh. I'm thinking, *For all you know.*

And then, for reasons I still fail to understand, I look at the clock, which gives us an hour and a half to wait, probably longer, and before I really know how, I'm climbing into the cab of his truck. You can't complain there are no knights in shining armor if you don't even give them a chance, right?

Dear Boyan,

It seemed to me as I stood alone at the roadside, seventeen miles from the nearest town, that I should have known I was not going to reach you. The guy's hand on my leg while he jerked off at the wheel had left me feeling scathed. If that's a word. His truck was carrying a load of molded plastic swimming pools. That was the only funny part. And this thing I have for heroes . . . Maybe I have a man problem as much or even worse than I have a plastics addiction. After I bit him and he finally stopped to let me out, I crossed the highway and walked back along the weedy median in the direction of town as it started to rain.

The first guy I ever slept with, it was almost platonic. Well, I should say something old-fashioned like "chaste." His name was Jimmy Ray, and he talked me into taking my shirt off and letting him stay with me in my single bed in the staff quarters at the Children's Home over in Perry County where I was trying to win souls. We kissed a lot and held each other, and I fell asleep on his big, padded chest—the two of us shirtless in the sweltering Kentucky heat. I was still living a life of holiness then, and he always stopped when I said we needed to. All the nights after that, I'd climb the outdoor stairs of the house where he lived with his granny—she fast asleep down below—and I'd stay with him in that wide bed in the big upstairs room. I'd sleep beside him. It was a lot for me and enough, it seemed, for him, just lying there. Especially since he already had a girlfriend in Berea. I always left before daylight.

But here's the thing, Boyan. Jimmy Ray was the pride of the town. A good boy who'd gone off to college at Berea then come back home to live with his granny. He spent his days taking the juvenile delinquents at the Methodist Children's Home, where I worked, down to swim in the lake. Not many kids from Perry County ever went away, and when they did, they rarely came back.

He worked in the mines, too, and I watched him down at the lake some evenings, lathering up and plunging into the blackened suds with the other men of the town after his shift. I don't know what made him such a local hero. Maybe just that he knew something of the developed world and chose that poor, beautiful shithole to live in.

Dear BS,

It's Tuesday. Somewhat miraculously, I'm home again. Am I lying to myself? My mother (a psychologist, you may remember) is sure that I am. "What's with the long face?" she says. She is hosing off Aldo's plastic geraniums. This would make me laugh if I didn't believe she posed a serious planetary threat.

"Where to begin?" I say.

It's raining, Boyan, and all the vast space between me and where you are is opening up again. The hollers and the mountains are burping their plastic trash from Paducah to Pikeville and all the way to Newport News. The billboards are hollering salvation, but at this point I long only for the oblivious passive aggressions of the Piggly Wiggly parking lot. I have to admit, I'm losing faith. I want to not need a hero. Even a boy-hero. You are still a boy, really. But this is my hymn to sloppy ideals and ill-conceived plans.

"You heard about the pandemic?" my mother asks.

"Uh—no?"

"Then what?" She offers me an Adirondack chair—resin, not wood—and settles into one herself. She drops the hose at our feet. "They're calling for flash floods tonight," she says, looking at the dark sky to the south. "Leftovers from the hurricane coming up the coast."

She probably thought I would spill, but I withheld. She couldn't fix this. Suddenly, I got what I wouldn't even call an idea. It was more like an urge that I interpreted as an inspiration.

After my mom went to bed, the rain kept up, battering the grass and forming a gully-wash that turned her chair on its side and moved it along the yard until a leg caught on something. I watched it from the dining room window. The rain felt like a big sigh. Or a shower at the end of a long day.

I started with the smaller items—the plastic pots she'd left on the stoop after planting the real geraniums, the key chains and refrigerator magnets with messages of hope or someone else's vacation highlights. I wanted the flood to come. I wanted the action to be big. I threw it all out into the gully-wash and watched it trip and stutter down the lawn toward the McNaughtons' place. As the gully widened and got deeper, I threw in the melamine dinner plates—the sunflower ones I'd gathered from the kitchen—along with the trash bags and sandwich bags. It felt good to purge that house of its plastic legacy and of all the false satisfactions it had brought my mother and me.

I love my mother, I do. But I carried out the Tupperware cake storage container too. I opened the lid and offered what was left of the Lady Baltimore cake to the rain. It was only half gone, since I'd been away for most of a day. The cover floated off on a rivulet while I watched the cake shed its frosting and turn into a sponge, then splurge and split on its Tupperware base.

Was this the way to a better world? In retrospect, I have to say no. But it seemed so as I hauled up the Legos and the baby dolls from the basement. Then I put out the shower curtain and the desk lamp and the electric column fan and a bunch of other stuff, as if setting up a yard sale. A few inches of rain take the whole lot! And because a deluge is no time for delusions, I took the unsent letters to you, rolled them up, and released them in plastic water bottles. Signed, Milly.

In the wee hours of my purge, my mother came out.

"What in the name of God?" she cried, her bottle-dyed hair glowing an alarmist red under the backyard spotlight she'd turned on before dashing through the screen door in her nightie. I couldn't see her face, but I didn't need to. The yard was already flooding, and the cake holder swirled around the flagpole like an insurrection. A computer keyboard and a mega-size liquid-Tide jug battered my mother's shins when she turned toward me. We don't use Tide, so I knew some stuff was coming down from the Brausers' place. There was something very beautiful about it, more direct than a letter, these artifacts en route to the Great Pacific Garbage Patch. And just as I thought that, I realized a terrible thing. It was all headed to the Atlantic. Because of the watershed. Stuff washed from here down to the Ohio River and then out to the Atlantic. Not to your giant filters. Not to you at all, Boyan. "Come back!" I shouted to my mother.

"What have you done?" she screamed.

"I'm facing up to the truth!" I cried. Because it was a lie, indeed, all of that plastic. "Maybe it's time for you to do the same! It feels almost biblical, doesn't it?" Then, angry and a little crazed, I added, "This is my letter to the world!" Emily Dickinson, who I hadn't thought of since the sixth grade, sounded good just then. But almost as soon as I said it, I was sorry. Because it was then that my mother lost her footing.

In trying to fetch the Tupperware that was caught in the forsythia at the bottom of the yard, she had headed downstream. Plowing toward her through water up past my knees and all that floating debris, I saw her fall.

This is my letter to the world / That never wrote to me.

In the beginning there were no words. There were no letters. Just things happening. Acts of God, or whatever. In the beginning, Boyan Slat, you were just a boy diving in the crystal blue-green Aegean in Greece and bummed to find so much plastic. Trash at the bottom of everything. It all came down to you. You were only seventeen when you dropped out of the university to build your magnificent filtration system, predicting that within five years you could clean up fifty percent of the plastic trash in the ocean. Peace out, Boyan!

I admit I always thought the world at the bottom of the lake was paradise. Our drowned town. Maybe it was dirty and full of failures, its own dead end. Maybe what I did the other night was about wanting to go back. And since I'm all about the truth right now, here's a tidbit: Boyan Slat, you never wrote to me either. Maybe you couldn't. I don't know.

I went out and got my mother. I don't want to make a big deal of it, how I had to rescue her. Because she got kind of banged up last night, and it was after two in the morning when I helped her limp upstairs, her arm around my neck.

The water had gone down by the time I got up this morning, and all our stuff was gone. Our forsythias and our whole lawn are now decorated generously with the neighbors' plastic.

My mother calls out to me in the yard, where I am checking things for the recycling symbol. "Where is the coffee maker?"

For a long, uncomfortable moment, I find I can't speak. She throws up her hands.

"I'll take you out for coffee," I say. "We'll get chocolate croissants at Butterfingers."

My mother and I both went under for a few seconds last night. That's right. I fell too, trying to rescue her, and I felt the water swirl around me like doomsday around the knees of the poor, sad, deluded ones.

"What you did last night was pretty stupid," my mother says. "And a little deranged. What was your point? Are you angry with me and your father for splitting up?"

Jesus, Boyan. She still doesn't get it. "Maybe," I say.

Dear Boyan,

What I loved most about religion—and yes, faith—was 1) The singing, and 2) The unguarded optimism, which came through in the singing. Maybe also having a man in charge 3) *My Jesus, I love thee; I know thou art mine. For thee, all the glories of sin I resign. I love thee for wearing the thorns on thy brow. If ever I loved thee* . . . By this point, Boyan, I might just as well be singing about you—sole hope for the planet's redemption. If ever I loved thee, *tis now*. Tis now.

I'm supposedly working on registration for summer courses at Morehead State. But instead, I'm sitting in the living room surfing the five channels you get on TV with no cable. On one is local news about a mother who murdered her two toddlers. I flip to the national news, where refugees are washing ashore on a Greek island, and piles of rubber dinghies and life vests are destroying the landscape. Rubber isn't plastic, is it? I mean, I think it's better. Natural. But still, disposal is a problem. Then back to local coverage on the planned ethane cracker plant along the Ohio River. The reporter says it's part of the growing vision for an Appalachian Plastics Hub. The region will lead the country in the manufacture of plastic pellets, to be used in the manufacture of what I can't bear to hear, so I turn the TV off.

To tell you the truth, I thought it would always be like it was with Jimmy Ray. But I found out later you couldn't just trust people and expect . . . I don't know. That you could control what happened. Bad things happened, they did. To me. And whose fault was that? I think probably mine. The fault of the girl who still believed, only not enough.

After the summer I worked at the Children's Home on my mission stint, things went not just a little bit haywire. The director made advances toward a seventeen-year-old girl to whom he'd been like a father. The son of the preacher over in Chavies shocked everyone by wanting a sex-change operation. Also, Twyla Combs' father, Jimmy Ray's next-door neighbor, shot himself in the head out on the front stoop because the miners were out of work. I heard that Jimmy Ray went to work for management at one of the mines. Management wasn't too popular.

Boyan, I am, apparently, nothing like you. Everything I try to do confirms that I'm an impulsive idealist who will not change the world.

Maybe I should stop trying before somebody really gets hurt.

Dear Boyan,

I've been in my room for a couple of days now, and I find no reason to leave. Can't help it after my epic fail. Did you ever read *The Odyssey*? I have it here on my bookshelf from sophomore year.

In a way, it's just about a series of bad calculations—a world stacking up to a homecoming and a violent conclusion. Also about lopsided relationships, and, of course, heroism. The parts I like best are when Odysseus tells his tales to Alcinous, the Phaeacian king, probably exaggerating but moving everybody to tears anyhow. The seeds of what happens next are always there in the story, in what happened before. Nausicaa has found the hero on the beach and secreted him away. She can't keep him there, and she can't really ride on his shirttails, but she is part of the story. She finds him broken and shows him a little love. Myth is only mythic when it travels from mouth to ear, connecting people across a treacherous geography. It's fed by the telling.

I never had a sword, or diving gear, or even a hearth. And for sure nobody like you sitting around listening to me ramble.

I'm not done with this letter, but I have to get my lazy ass over to the high school, where I'm coaching the girls track team. Did I mention that I've never competed in a track event? It's a good thing I don't get paid. I've watched a few YouTube videos to see how it's done—hurdles, sprints, the mile. Dear God, I'm ridiculous. And the team. They are dreadfully bad. I pray for rain—heavy rain—when we have the meet over in Hazard. My prayers will probably go unanswered, and the girls will lose every event, but at least I'm not abusing them as I suspect their former coach was.

Boyan,

Yesterday, when I get home, my mother stops me in the kitchen and says, "Who's Boyan Slat and do I get to meet him?"

I say, "So you've been in my room?"

She says she was putting away the clothes she washed for me, thank you very much, and she couldn't help seeing what was on my laptop, which I had left open. She sits down at the table, looking exhausted.

"I don't even send them anymore," I say. "I don't know why I keep writing them."

"You know, your father wanted to write. To be a writer. But instead, he was an engineer. You know he worked on the dam that flooded our town?"

"He wouldn't do that," I say.

"He did. It was his job. Army Corps of Engineers. He'd do that during the day and then come home and read Aldo Leopold and John Muir and Rachel Carson at night."

"Isn't that what you call cognitive impairment?"

"Dissonance. Cognitive dissonance."

"So he had, like, zero impact on the environment, except for that?"

"You're just like him. Only the opposite. You go around trying to engineer solutions—but what's really happening are the words. You actually write. Your father never did. And I'm glad you weren't involved in building the dam, after your little demonstration last week," she says, smiling and wiping a pile of coffee cake crumbs into her hand, then getting up to dump them.

I give her a look.

"I'm just saying," she says.

Now I'm thinking about yesterday. Because it was our last track meet and there were no awards to be given out for a series of losses and failures, the girls sent their beloved coach home with a small gift. I'm glad I didn't open it in front of them. It was a silver pendant, about the size of a quarter, and in engraved script it said *Couch*.

Maybe my mother was right. I wasn't so much cut out for action. Though we all need heroes. In some weird way, maybe I was theirs.

The next day, also weirdly, one of my letters to you turned up in the *Eastern Kentucky Herald*. Apparently, the bottle I'd put it in floated down and landed in a flower pot at Gill Nasaka's house, and he works in the print room, but he took it to the editor, who printed it with the columns. Then two other people found messages in bottles downstream from here and took them to the paper.

They're looking for this "Milly," the writer. Should I turn myself in? I mean, I guess I don't know why I wouldn't. Or what they would want from me. If you put a message in a bottle and someone gets it, then do you owe them the courtesy of not giving up on saving the planet?

I found some marigold seeds in the basement, and I'm going to plant them on Aldo Leopold's grave since his plastic geraniums washed away. I'll just see if the seeds are still good. And it's been a long time since I wrote my father. This is probably my last letter to you, Boyan—if it even is a letter.

I don't believe, anymore, in being born again. I think that's what people do when they're afraid or they desperately need another chance. Still, it's not naive to think I am capable of good. Or that there is good in the world. You have given me permission to think so. And it seems that even my sorry, misdirected, impulsive action might one day lead to good. I'm not sure what I was looking for this whole time, Boyan. I'm not stalking you, or worshipping you, or wooing you. Though I admit the letters were kind of personal, there's something epic in my heart and I'm just trying to let it play.

The Slight

The Sahara it is not. At night, the little tourist caravan arrives at a wave of dunes cresting beneath the starry sky. But during the day, they carry on through splotches of the unvaried scrub that is Rajasthan's Thar. Trees are occasional, of a variety that gives the camels gas and causes them to slobber greenly. They meet almost no one and only occasionally come to a well, into which Hameed or one of the two other camel drivers lowers a bucket. The sun is hot, even in February. The desert smell is dry. It ends abruptly in the olfactories, no moisture to carry it. But at night, the camp smells of canvas and ticking that has been rolled all day; and then the dry fire makes its thin but persuasive argument almost without smoke. Readily, it flares up.

There are four tourists in the caravan now: the American, tanned and angular; the stubble-faced South African and his scorched wife; and the couple's small daughter, who rides confidently alone. They approach a village of thatched huts where the dirt is well swept, but no women or children come to gawk at the foreigners on camels. They are greeted, instead, by a man of the village in a soiled white shirt. He saunters out and enters into a brusque-sounding altercation with the camel drivers. It is five or ten minutes before

Hameed is able to satisfy the man, and he signals to the tourists that it is time to move on.

Later, when they stop at a gnarled acacia tree for lunch, the American, Amelia, asks Hameed on behalf of the other tourists what the argument was about. All of them are worried that they may have intruded on the village. Hameed says there is to be a feast in the village that evening. The man in the white shirt was cooking a goat, and he had invited them.

"But he sounded angry," she says.

"He was unhappy that we would not come," Hameed tells her.

It is the American's fourth day. The South African couple, Wes and Nicky, along with their eight-year-old daughter, Hannah, were driven out by jeep to join the caravan the previous morning, as arranged at Amelia's own insistence. She hadn't wanted to be alone with the camel drivers when the brothers from Rio left the trek on the third day. Wes and Nicky are as relieved as she is to know that they were not unwelcome in the village. They trust that Hameed, as head of their expedition, will not take them where they are not wanted. Though disappointed that they will miss out on an authentic experience with desert people, Amelia supposes Hameed has his reasons.

When he hears their wistful comments at the mention of goat meat after a steady diet of vegetable curry, Hameed offers them the option of buying some goat from the man in the village, meat that he and his nephew will prepare for dinner. Eagerly, the group collects funds. Their buying and eating the goat will feel a bit like gratitude for the hospitality extended. Though in truth it is hard for Amelia to reconcile this story with the irritation they witnessed in the man from the village.

After the negotiations at the camp, the message sent to the nearby village of huts, the payment, and the anticipation of a meal for carnivores; after the departure of the old driver with the prodigious white mustache and his return with sticks for the fire and goat milk he has collected from nobody knows where; when the Westerners have rested and washed themselves for dinner and the camel drivers have cooked the goat in one big pot, Amelia and the South Africans sit in the sand near the fire to eat. And the goat meat, which they have paid for as a delicacy—a savory, carnal satisfaction—the goat they are served from the long-watched pot, is nothing but impenetrable gristle and bone.

The day looks like this: either they have come to a remote village, little visited, and been welcomed as friends, as guests, but have refused that welcome and have now paid to be disappointed in addition. Or they have trespassed on a village, been evicted, and have been placated by a lie, which the current mouthful of gristle was meant to substantiate. Either way, there's a story to be told. Amelia will sleep hungry, but there is India, Rajasthan, a bevy of camels drooling green dreams under a crystalline night sky. It's only appetite. And maybe only hers. She cannot tell, in the firelight, how the others have fared.

The drivers will eat, as always, when the tourists have finished. They will add the fiery peppers to what is left. When they do and begin eating, Wes asks them, "Hot, is it?"

"You want to try?" says Hameed, also known to tourists as Ali Baba, though Amelia and the others prefer to call him by his name. He is handsome, his features browned and angular, his eyes kind. Wes agrees, handing his tin plate to Hameed, who gives him a lump of goat. They all watch as Wes puts the fork into his mouth and begins to chew.

"Amelia," he says to the American, "you must try this."

"Not too hot?" she says.

"Have a little," he repeats, and he hands her the plate. The meat is succulent, tender. Tasting it, she is less certain than ever of her place in this coded universe.

*

She beds down in the thick roll of pads and blankets they have prepared for her and as she is trying to not ask *why* or *how* but rather merely to *be*, Wes comes and sits in the sand next to her head. She props herself up on an elbow. "We paid for that goat," he says, his voice a small conspiracy in the dark, "and they kept the best cuts for themselves."

"It was dark," she says. "Maybe they couldn't see."

"It's not the first time they've cooked a goat," he says.

The drivers had been deferentially considerate the three days she had been with them before the South Africans arrived. They had waited, each meal, until she and the brothers from Rio were finished eating before they added the peppers and then ate whatever remained. They had even offered the tourists seconds. Amelia tells Wes that she trusts the drivers completely. And besides, it was dark when they were cooking.

"I'm going to demand the money back," Wes says.

"Ask for your share if you want," she tells him.

That night she sleeps fitfully, less on account of the goat than of Wes, and in her sleeplessness, she adjusts the lighting on the cooking pot all night. Had there been more moon? Less moon? But how? There are no clouds in the desert. The moon is full.

She wakes to the sound of Wes and Nicky bickering a small way beyond the dunes where they have slept. Before tea and toast, which the drivers are preparing over the fire, he comes to her again.

While the rest of them slept, taking refuge under the night full of stars, his anger continued to blister. His face looks worked over, his wavy auburn hair anarchic. He has gnashed his teeth not just for one night, Amelia thinks. She recognizes the wincing avoidance of his wife, who keeps their child close to her in an alliance of two. They have been through Thailand and Laos with him, have most likely weathered his sense of justice. His refusals to be had. And now, he has come to a decision: he will call the tour operator on his mobile and ask for another leader. They eat in silence. He doesn't drink his tea.

As they are loading the camels, Hameed comes to help her with her pack and her bedding and asks what's wrong with the South African. He is dismayed to hear their perception of the meat. That they had saved the best for themselves. He will happily pay them back. "We are whoever you believe we are," he says, with submissive irony.

"I don't want the money," she says.

"Why not?" says Hameed.

"I don't understand what happened, exactly," she tells him. "Because what Wes says is true. We had nothing but gristle and bones. And the meat you had was really, really good."

"How did it happen?" she asks.

"We do not think in this way," Hameed says.

They ride across the desert: an American, three offended Muslims, and an angry South African whose family looks to be on the verge of dissolution. They are all counting on Amelia, but what does she know? Only how ugly they as tourists must be to those they pay to amuse them. And that Hameed has the flatbread smell of a man who has been baked on desert hardpan, where everything is cleaner. She likes the smell of him. The last thing an American in the full bloom of her ignorance should attempt in the desert is an act of diplomacy. Still, she extracts from Wes a reluctant promise not to act immediately. She asks that he think about it awhile, consider the impact on livelihoods were he to phone in a complaint.

Amelia has plenty of time to think about it too, and when she does, she has to trust Hameed and his nephew blindly, since they have offered no explanation for what happened the night before, but rather only an apology that the tourists had felt slighted. The moon's a thousand watts overhead at night, and there in the desert, Amelia feels like Emerson's transparent eyeball, aware of the whole universe in the moment. In spite of everything, she feels that it is good, though she cannot understand it fully. She has watched the dry pooling of the camels' feet over the sand, has looked into their soft eyes, seen the great lids close and open again. She feels stripped down like a thorn tree, is capable of loving water. She would eat beetles if they were prepared with a kind heart. She would eat mice.

When they stop for lunch just beyond a village the next day, only Hameed stays by the fire cooking. Amelia, Wes, Nicky, and the girl, Hannah, wait beneath a tree for their food. The quiet of the camp is ruptured by a loud, dismal hubbub—an ornery animal complaint. They run to the edge of the bluff to see: surrounded by the other drivers and a couple of men apparently from a village nearby, two camels are kneeling below, awkwardly engaged. The men helping them with the mechanics of their humping shout their instructions to one another like a crew on a porn set. Later, Wes will say that their tour guides are moonlighting. Doing private business with their camels as studs on company time. This will fuel his resentments. But Amelia watches with fascination the agonized architecture of camel sex. It is a construction she has never even tried to imagine. She catches Hameed, a few yards away, watching her watching, and he looks back at the fire. How strange to think that instinct and intuition are not enough in this situation. She is aware that hers are currently being shaped by the mating operation, the sounds of which dominate the landscape and the air around her. They are being shaped skillfully by Hameed as he squats by the fire and shows her how to use the heel of her hand to shape roti from flour and water. She wishes that she had come alone with Hameed. Things would have been much easier.

And then, eating rice and potato curry, mopping her plate with roti, she understands how incidental she and the South Africans really are—how they have been allowed into this thread of the story but have no place there, though they have, indeed, paid to ride in thrilling silhouette on the backs of gainly animals. It is embarrassing how many times during the meal they are asked, "Is the food OK? How is everything?" She despises the new deference on demand.

The next morning, the old man with the tufted white mustache goes out, his bottle empty, and returns with it half full. Hameed's nephew says the old one goes out to milk a goat. But whose goat has he been milking? When he goes off like that, Amelia has *Lawrence of Arabia* visions of bedouins with pistols, shooting at whoever tries to drink at their well. But the old one has not been shot, and he drinks the milk like a baby. Drinks it all, as usual, offering none to anyone. Wes glances in the old man's direction, then gives Amelia a look that says, "Exhibit B."

"Do you drink goat's milk?" Amelia asks Wes.

"Maybe I do," he replies. "I would. My daughter would."

Amelia herself does, actually. She wonders what it tastes like fresh and warm, which complicates her position.

That day, when they ride on and Amelia begins to feel tingly in the heat, Hameed stops to wet her scarf at a well and wraps her head in it, turban style. He is teaching her the ways of the desert. Wes, unassisted, is looking puffy. His wife gives him a handful of pills and tells him to drink more water. The girl, Hannah, rides bravely on her own, afraid only at the dismount, when the camel, in the process of kneeling, lurches and jolts precariously, sending her sliding down toward its neck.

The desert reduces each of them to a camel's baggage. Seeing the exotic shadows they make on the sand, Amelia thinks they could be anyone. They could be thousands of years ago, or as far into the future. The sun darkens the faces even of the Westerners, and their turbans and cotton tunics erase identities. But there's a nerve that's rubbed raw by exposure, by dependency, a nerve on the alert—which maybe too is ancient. The world of bush, sand, magnificent sun is *where* they are, and maybe it doesn't much matter *who* or *when*. But the nerve makes them finicky and alive. It's a *how*. And even when they are well watered and protected, it tingles with hate or love or misery. It registers the smallest indignity. Even at night, lying under a bazillion stars, someone is feeling slighted.

When they stop for lunch, the old one goes out for his walkabout with the water bottle, and by the time he returns, the whole company's in a sulk. Wes has asked Hameed how many miles they have covered, and Hameed says he doesn't know. "Ten? Fifteen?" the South African presses him.

"We measure in days," Hameed says. "Two days since you arrived."

"Show me on the map," Wes says. "Look. Here's Jaisalmer. We came this far by jeep, right? And then where?"

Hameed, who has been tending a pot with diced onions and carrots and zucchini, takes the map from the other man's hand and drops it into the fire.

"I'll kill you," Wes says, nostrils flaring in contempt. "I swear by Christ on the bloody cross, I will kill you."

"It's an old map," Hameed replies calmly. "Out here, geography changes with the wind. The map bears no relation to our situation." This seems a ridiculous argument, and Wes attempts to rescue his map from the flames but succeeds only in scorching his hand. He pulls it back and mutters between clenched teeth, "Are you out of your bleeding mind?" He kicks sand into the fire and into Hameed's face. Sand flies into the pot Hameed is stirring. The pot that was everyone's lunch.

When Wes walks toward the thorn tree under which his wife and child have been dozing, Hameed, quietly emptying the pot of its gritty contents and wiping it clean, asks Amelia, "Why did you come here?"

Amelia doesn't know how to answer.

"Have you found what you were looking for?" Hameed asks.

She is surprised by the question and is spared her discomfort by some children who wander up to the camp: three of them, thin and dark, their eyes lined heavily with kohl against the sun. The oldest girl wears bangles, and the boy carries a small tape player which, once he has their attention, he quickly rewinds to a whining, sinuous melody the older girl, presumably his sister, can dance to. While the younger sister, only three or four, wanders freely around the site, curious and ignored, they all watch the nine- or ten-year-old, who moves with a fascinating sensuality. The boy looks bored until the song finishes. Then he snaps the recorder off and applauds, becoming again the impresario. He says in English, "You love it. She is very good, no?" and begins to ask for pens or rupees, but Hameed waves them off. The boy utters a friendly but disappointed sound through his lips, as if Hameed had ruined something that was pleasurable for all, and they move back off into the desert, hurrying for a couple of steps each time Hameed growls at them.

"So tell me, Amelia," Hameed insists, not willing to be distracted from his purpose. "What were you looking for?"

"I don't know," she says. "Sand and sky. Something real. Something true."

"But you paid for it," he says. "You pay, and it is not going to be real."

She knows he is right. And she is naive to think that perhaps she has made a friend, though Hameed does seem to like her. Is that perception merely part of what she has paid for? Or does he find her different somehow? Willing to put her hands into the flour and water and work the dough. And she can't help now remembering the way she felt when he watched her watching the camels. She wants to do something decisive to allay the tensions with the South Africans, but she wonders if her perceptive Emersonian eyeball has a gnat or a fly in it. The romantic notion of Hameed as a sheikh in *Lawrence of Arabia*. Her obscuring desire. Whatever she says or does will have the distinct potential for being the wrong thing. Even Gertrude Bell, "Queen of the Desert," unwittingly helped the British draw the geographic boundaries responsible for at least another century of conflict in the Middle East.

"Tell me, Hameed," she says. "Whose goats does the old one milk?"

"Ask him," Hameed says, indicating the other man with a nod.

As she suspected, the old one does not speak English. He looks at her with a furrowed brow when she questions him. Hameed repeats her question in Urdu, and the prodigious white tufts of the old one's mustache lift slightly like wings so she knows he is smiling.

The Thar stretches from the Rann of Kutch in the south to the Punjab Plain in the north, two hundred thousand square kilometers of it. At night, the tourists lie under the stars taking in the vastness of the universe. And whose goat is the old man milking? Hameed translates the answer: Always the same goat. His own.

Hameed smiles. Not to worry.

But circling the old man's goat?

If that's what they've been doing, they are going nowhere, and perhaps they have been made fools of. Or Hameed has simply been too busy catering to their tastes to take them farther into the scrubby Thar. This new information Amelia will not share with Wes, now that hostilities have come into the open. Already, there will be only rice for lunch.

Over at the place where the gear is stowed, Wes growls a torrent of curses. His cell phone has gone missing, and he is emptying the contents of his small pack onto the sand. Amelia walks over to help him search the area around their bags. "I need my phone," he says through his teeth, his rage barely controlled.

"The children were running around near our things," his wife calls out. "The smallest one was."

"If you saw that, why didn't you do something? We're already at the mercy of thieves," he says, loud enough for Hameed to hear.

Amelia sees that a large section of his hand has begun to blister from when he reached into the fire, and he tries to keep the sun off it by pulling his shirt cuff down. Hameed has not offered any first aid, and Wes will not ask for it. "Do you think you need medical attention?" she asks him.

"I need for him to admit that he's screwing us," he says. "Do you still not get that?"

"You're being unfair," she says. "What he says about the map may be true. People are nomadic here, aren't they? There's a lot we don't understand."

"Here's what you don't understand. He would rather be screwing you alone," he says. "Handsome Ali Baba."

"Is that really what you think?" she says, her uncertainty not fully disguised by scorn.

After a quiet and insufficient midday meal, as they are washing dishes together, Hameed tells Amelia, "Tomorrow morning, we will take you to the road where you will catch the bus for Ahmedabad." He says this with a somewhat tenuous authority, watching her face for a reaction. It has been her plan all along to go to Ahmedabad, though she'd expected to catch the bus in Jaisalmer.

"Are you going to take Wes and Nicky back to Jaisalmer?" Amelia says.

"They paid for real adventure. In miles. I thought they paid for safekeeping too," he says, scouring an already clean pan. "But they did not. I want to give them only what they paid for."

She can think only that Hameed will take the South Africans deeper into the Thar. Will what he gives them be more real than what he has withheld from her? It seems there are no instincts left for any of them to trust. Just the promptings of pride and injury, of intrigue and disaffection. The suspension of disbelief. That is what she chooses to trust.

The old driver and the nephew, she has learned, will not go on but will return to their village. Perhaps, like her, they are extras Hameed would rather not have to deal with. She hears them speaking in serious voices with him, as if trying to dissuade him and salvage his pride.

The next morning when she leaves for the bus, the camels are colicky from eating acacia trees. Hameed asks that a photo be taken of him with her on her camera before he sends her off at a gallop on camelback behind his nephew. He will depart alone with the South Africans. She imagines the sun relentless overhead, the ground shifting beneath the others as they go, landmarks and points of reference growing more elusive. Villagers even less friendly. The little caravan will follow Hameed into the consequences of the ignorance from which he may have tried to protect them—either his own or theirs. She will be shocked to discover how close to the road their route has actually been, in spite of the sense she has had of wandering in the barren wilderness. Hanging out the open door of the bus, from which she very well might fall to her death if two or three men grasping various parts of her body decide to release her, she will not be able to see the caravan at all behind the rise of sand and scrub at the edge of the road. She will tell this story, and the experience of it will seem true—her sailing down the highway, muslin salwar kameez billowing. The one arm that has found a bar to hold onto growing weak and threatening to let go, she has not yet begun to think of herself as an accomplice.

Feminine Mystique

"But when we sit together, close," said Bernard, "we melt into each other with phrases. We are edged with mist. We make an unsubstantial territory."
—VIRGINIA WOOLF, *The Waves*

1. The Evidence

FATHER ACACIUS: I found it in the orchard on the fifth of April, and now I place it on the table at supper as a lesson and a warning. The egg. It fairly well glows—its white shell nacreous in the candlelight. The brothers gather round. All silent. Some avert their eyes. The chicken comes before *and* after the egg, I say.

DEMETRIOS: Neither do we eat eggs nor keep any female domesticated animals at the monastery. Mount Athos is the Garden of the Virgin Mary. All that we do not do is in deference to her and to the mysteries she has bestowed on this place where once she walked.

SIMEON: Don't get me started. In my business, the order was clear: chicken, egg, omelet, and I used to make a mean pepper jack and mushroom. Which is to say a blessed one. That was in the old days.

BARSANUPHIUS: If I had ten euros for all the times I've seen that look on Brother Simeon's face, maybe I wouldn't even be here. While Father Acacius is providing his object lesson, Simeon is thinking what he could do with that egg. It's no secret that lack of employment inspired my taking orders. But I like it here, I do. Simeon, he ran a breakfast joint in Brooklyn, which he talks about nonstop but always out of range of Father Acacius. A big success, according to him. The order is his retirement.

PAUL: I can't stop looking. The egg is beautifully formed—a miracle of celestial engineering. For the moment it is the center of our little universe, and I understand, as I have always done, why the feminine is not allowed on Athos. No bitches, no hens. The feminine snags my spirit. Wily, it nudges me from within. Holy Mary, Mother of God, forgive me, a poor sinner.

DEMETRIOS: Father Acacius picks up the egg, holds it in the palm of his hand, and squeezing, crushes the shell and the yolk, letting the organic slime like the secret of life itself run down his closed fist onto the wooden table. It's like something from a mystic's dream.

FATHER ACACIUS (still fisted): In the name of the Father and of the Son.

BARSANUPHIUS: We go in peace. We go about our duties. Our vespers. We exhort one another for strength. We exorcise what demons are among us. We wonder at certain mysteries.

PAUL: And for all that is good, God be praised.

2. In the Garden

PAUL: It's morning in the garden. Sun on thistles at the border. Eggplants glistening in their skins. We eat by the grace of God and the labors of our hands.

BARSANUPHIUS: We discipline the body to free the spirit. We wake in the dark and loosen the soil with the hoe. Pull weeds. Is Romania my mother? Not in this other country of the spirit. This land dedicated to the Virgin. Who is my mother when my boots are in the dirt? It is spring and the spinach flourishes in rows like an illumination of the new day's text. Always the Virgin, our only mother. But her love is sterile. It is pure.

PAUL: From this garden of the Virgin, we are not cast out. We renounce the treachery of Eve and of women. The Virgin alone lives here among us on this Holy Mountain, our gift to her. Blessed and sanctified is she, who gives no cause for us to revile her, eternally virgin and shameless. I renounce the dreams engendered by the flesh. Which I dream nightly. Holy Mary, Mother of God, pray for us.

BARSANUPHIUS: We cut the spinach with shears, but some varmint has eaten the leaves from the end of the row. I study the situation.

SIMEON: Barsanuphius has taken his vows, but only as a last resort because he couldn't make it on the outside. He's not Greek either. Romanian. He's over there leaning on his shovel, observing, which he does a lot. The order isn't for everyone. I don't judge him, but God will judge. Or Father Acacius, who pokes his head out of the kitchen door at the very moment Brother Barsanuphius resumes digging. Always. Father Acacius is never quite in time to see how things really are. You can't retire until you've worked. I was good at what I did. I had a wife too, a necessary indulgence in my younger days.

BARSANUPHIUS: Brothers, I think we have a rabbit problem.

SIMEON: I sigh, put down my hoe to match Barsanuphius's easy posture, then walk over to take a look at the spinach. I stoop to examine the stems, which have been left. I jump back when a flash of purple on the ground beneath the unpicked leaves catches my eye. At first, I think it's a lizard or a small snake. But no. It's a hair elastic, like the ones we monks use, only ours are black. I pick it up from the dirt to show the others. In my experience, rabbits don't wear these.

BARSANUPHIUS: I didn't see at first, but there is a track two narrow feet have left in the soft soil. Bare feet.

PAUL: If the female of the species were allowed here, it would be the end of the order—the end of our spiritual orientation. I'm not saying it's their fault. I'm not saying it isn't. But women in the garden have been trouble from Day One.

BARSANUPHIUS: Holy Virgin, Intercessor compassionate and kind, forever pure, for you we forsake all things feminine, every trifle of sensual knowledge. I send the little elastic flying into the weeds.

SIMEON: Brother Paul smashes an almond blossom with the heel of his boot. There's something in the air.

3. Something in the Air

DEMETRIOS: Since its appearance, that elastic Barsanuphius sent zinging from the garden has, like the egg, permeated every moment of the day, as if the air around us, sterilized during a long, pestilential winter, had begun to traffic again in the germs common to humanity. After a long frost, the microclimates of the soul are reemerging.

BARSANUPHIUS: We're all unnerved by the incident in the garden. But then Simeon comes to me and says he needs my advice. As in wants my help. Which is, to put it mildly, a reversal. Is he being sarcastic? He says I'm perceptive. I think outside the box. He admits he's considered that a defect until now. (We are a religious order, after all. We promote life in the box for the liberation of the spirit.) He wants to know my opinion on the reintroduction of omelets to the menu for guests to the monastery. Pilgrims. Simeon, I say, I bet they miss you back in Brooklyn. Are you sure you were called to this life?

DEMETRIOS: I'm in the garden, and I sit down between the spinach and the cucumber plants and unlace my boots. I scroll my sodden socks away from my heels and free my toes, which evolve from their crumpled estate and, almost of their own accord, burrow into the loam. A fine morning mist has my hair dripping. My body is a shoot, and I feel close to God. I know how close I am has nothing to do with how I feel. I know the earth is not my mother. But its femininity is undeniably glorious today.

FATHER ACACIUS: If one artery is blocked, the whole body suffers a heart attack. I suspect a female presence on the mountain of the Holy Virgin.

DEMETRIOS: But if one brother is infused with the spirit, do not all breathe deeply?

FATHER ACACIUS: They may breathe hard, but not deeply.

4. Father Acacius' History Lesson

FATHER ACACIUS: The last time the sanctuary of Athos was breached by a woman was in 1929. One cross-dressing Miss Europe—a Greek beauty queen. And you all know what happened then.

ALL: We stare silently at our hands, folded in our laps, because, frankly, we don't. Our curiosity is aroused at the Abbott's own suggestion. As far as we know, nothing happened.

FATHER ACACIUS: The Great Hen Massacre of 1932. Against the moral laxity represented by excess feminine fowl. Gender-inspector monks were stationed at the port of Daphne.

ALL: Oh.

FATHER ACACIUS: There was also, around that time, the French journalist and philosophical writer Maryse Choisy, who cut off her primary sexual characteristic appendages in elective surgery to complete her disguise and spent a month undetected among the monks on Athos.

SIMEON: If a tree falls in the wood and no one hears it, does it make a sound?

FATHER ACACIUS: I know you hear it. Just look at your faces. And you know what it means.

DEMETRIOS (silent): The great mysteries continue to open?

BARSANUPHIUS (silent): We are more fully alive?

PAUL (silent): Perhaps we are afraid of who we are not?

SIMEON: It's just tradition, right? This thing about no women? It's not scriptural or anything, is it? I mean, where does it say? And she didn't make omelets, did she? This Choosy Mary?

ALL: Father Acacius puts us in spiritual lockdown against what devilment might be afoot.

DEMETRIOS: I dream Father Acacius presents to us the preserved breasts of a newly sainted Maryse Choisy. Not to kiss them, we bow our heads in reverence. But some visitors to the Holy Mountain are there and they do. Kiss the decamped breasts. And I am wondering in the dream, how did the breasts come to Athos? How did they make it past the gender-inspector monks at Daphne?

PAUL: The unadulterated maleness of noon among my brothers has ceased to be a comfort.

DEMETRIOS: I dream of refugees from Syria on the shores of Lesbos. They arrive in punctured rafts. In my dream, the women alone are turned back in rough seas.

5. Even the Virgin Stops Listening

PAUL: I ask for her help, and it's like talking to a wall. The wall must be in me. I confess this to Father Acacius and he says perhaps she does hear, but we are not worthy of her response, distracted as we have been by recent events. This makes no sense to me since we know we have never been worthy. We have never been worth listening to. We with our body odors and our gripes and our ceaseless desires. Our tireless renunciation of all of the above.

DEMETRIOS: We do what we have done for a thousand years.

PAUL: Dear ordinary life. Dear ordinary days. Oh, gravity of men's voices at Evensong. Voices of clarity in the gendered dawn. There was a time when it felt like enough. It was everything.

FATHER ACACIUS: In the refectory the brothers argue over the horta with lemon. (Are they overcooked? Should it matter whether they are or not?) They argue over our neighbors, the monks of Esphigmenou, who have been excommunicated for their views on the calendar and the relationship between the Ecumenical Patriarch and the Pope. Then the brothers argue over the calendar. Julian vs. Gregorian. The moon comes up, full and bright, and they put aside their differences before bed. But we're responsible for the traditions alive in us a thousand years. I am sore afraid.

BARSANUPHIUS: Father Acacius says to me, as I am stirring a batch of chocolate in the auxiliary kitchen, monitoring the temperature with care, that he senses I am unhappy. He has come in suddenly to find me at my work, where I belong at ten a.m. and where he does not belong. Unhappy?

FATHER ACACIUS: It's a simple question. Are you unhappy?

BARSANUPHIUS: What in the devil is he talking about? We seek not to be buffeted by ordinary passions.

FATHER ACACIUS: Though maybe I'm doing a little reconnaissance, I've really no idea what makes me go there and talk the way

I do. I do not tell him stories of the Desert Fathers or speak in parables as usual. Something's wrong, I say.

BARSANUPHIUS: Do you question my spiritual condition?

FATHER ACACIUS: Call it intuition.

BARSANUPHIUS: I know that feelings are not to be trusted, Father, whether they're mine or yours.

FATHER ACACIUS: So it's true?

BARSANUPHIUS: I miss my sisters. Terribly now. I say this, and all of his uncharacteristic empathy turns to reprimand.

FATHER ACACIUS: You will say the Jesus Prayer to quell your dangerous nostalgia. Otherwise, you will remain silent for the rest of the week.

6. The Counting of the Linens

BARSANUPHIUS: At meals, we wipe the oil and tomato from our lips with napkins made of flax, woven by our brothers in Romania. Our days are measured out in prayer and labor and in keeping our mouths clean during the dinner lesson. I try not to miss Romania. The napkins were a gift. I miss the laughter of girls outside my old monastery in Bucharest. But only in moments, heard from the open window in March. And not because I want from it anything beyond the crisp, sweet edge of the laughter itself, like that of a lettuce leaf. But some of the napkins have gone missing. Brother Simeon took them from the line this morning and folded them.

DEMETRIOS: Did he count them when he hung them to dry?

SIMEON: I never count them. There's no need to count them.

DEMETRIOS: There are not enough to go around at midday. Four brothers are without napkins.

SIMEON: Four brothers whose greasy socks I'll have to wash.

FATHER ACACIUS: Some menace is afoot. Some she-devil.

PAUL: We know her presence among us. We know, too, that our privilege is at a cost to those we have kept out from this garden.

BARSANUPHIUS: Stirring our chocolate, baking our bread, arguing in the passageways, we miss the empathy of women.

DEMETRIOS: The breeze speaks our names, nostalgic for the feminine in us. We have distilled our spirits like heavy proof alcohol. It tastes like disinfectant.

BARSANUPHIUS: The wash on the clothesline flutters in the dark beneath the moon, our habits and our linens. It ghosts our daytime activities, swims bodiless in the air, suggesting all we cannot see.

FATHER ACACIUS: We will lay a trap for the thief of our contentment. Our certainties. I suggest chocolate. We refrain from eating the chocolate we produce. Only a female can't resist it—a carnal creature with a soul. The wild boars will leave it alone.

BARSANUPHIUS: If there is a female intruder on the mountain, the trap will find her. I pray that it does not. My sisters are crazy for chocolate. When I was a novice, I was cleansed of my nostalgia, my passions, my memories, even my relationships. I forgot and forgave the sound of the laughter of girls. Even my mother's love. I pray for the Virgin's intercession.

7. The Trap

PAUL: The Virgin's love is a sterile love. It purges us. She empties out our hearts to fill them with the Holy Spirit. She returns us to a natural state of detachment. So why do I wake each day to daylight and see yesterday as a wasteland—like a landscape ravaged not by industry and enterprise but by our manly fears? We are men dwelling in the sterile love of the Virgin. The Virgin who won't even talk to us anymore. Who refuses to carry our messages to God.

DEMETRIOS: We leave the chocolate and post the watch. We compete for the assignment of staying out all night under the feminine pull of the moon.

FATHER ACACIUS: Father, forgive me, but I cannot tell them that she has started talking back to me. Not as in answering, but as in remonstrating. She says she misses the company of women. She once asked for the Holy Mountain of Athos, yes, but not to share it only with hundreds of bearded men. Thousands of men. If I speak these words aloud, we will be excommunicated, like the monks at Esphigmenou, farther north. We will have to barricade ourselves in and fight the police. I can't trust her anymore, talking back this way.

BARSANUPHIUS: My sister, in the afternoon, reading under the orange trees. She is reading Kafka. She is reading Cavafy. A poem about a man cherishing a bloody bandage from the man he secretly loves—surprisingly beautiful and sad. She's reading Jung too. I miss her with the Jesus Prayer. Lord Jesus Christ have mercy on me, a sinner. She looks up from her book with a half-smile, suggesting she knows half a world I don't. Animus. Anima. But this is not my story.

FATHER ACACIUS: It is a story of the brotherhood—a cautionary tale—of how we came to believe there was a feminine presence on the Holy Mountain of Athos. And of how, the very night we set the trap, we caught the culprit.

SIMEON: A bearded, Arab-looking man—eyes like lightning and a brow like a thunderbolt. He spoke no Greek. No English. He seemed lost—was hungry and cold, so we took him, against his will, and gave him a room and fed him.

ACACIUS: His food disappears quickly at supper, and he repairs to his room. I confess that in my certainty of a female presence on the mountain, even I had let intuition run away with me.

DEMETRIOS: I go early in the morning to wake him for matins, but he is not there, the bedclothes undisturbed. There is nothing but a scrap of pink on the floor just beneath the bed where he must have sat. I cross the threshold and bend to pick it up—a small pink tin. On top is the face of a kitten wearing a bow. When I twist the cap, a strawberry aroma wafts up like incense to my olfactories.

PAUL: At breakfast, Father Acacius places a coquettish pink tin on the table. Exhibit B. Or C, depending on how you count. The cap is on, so we are exposed only to the feminine splash of color in the eye, not the odiferous pleasantry of the contents. Father Acacius allows us to ponder it for the duration of our repast. If there really is trouble in this paradise, why am I calmer in my spirit? And why do I wrestle less with the flesh? To hide this feeling, I adopt my expressionless monk face with just a bit of disdain, which I hope passes for discernment. The tin asserts its innocence.

BARSANUPHIUS: He must have put the little balm in his pocket for her. There was no place to keep it because she was wearing a dress. Or was he, indeed, alone? Was he carrying it to remember what he had lost? He said his name was Ahmad. Even a Muslim would do such a thing. Especially a Muslim? Our speculation goes unspoken.

8. The Revelation at the Cave

PAUL: When our little delegation finds him, he is not far from the sea, camped out in a cave near the olive grove. He doesn't run when we approach but comes out to meet us, turning once to the cave with a gesture that says, "Stay there."

DEMETRIOS: Hanging from the limb of an olive tree are two battered orange life jackets, along with three white cloth napkins.

BARSANUPHIUS: We are trying to communicate, asking in Greek and Russian, Romanian and English, where he comes from and what he is doing here. He answers in what must be Arabic. At a loss, Paul produces the little lip balm for the intruder to see, holding the tin up between his thumb and his forefinger in such a way that it eclipses the morning sun, still low in the sky.

PAUL: The Arab hesitates a long moment before calling over his shoulder in the direction of the cave.

DEMETRIOS: I dreamt of the refugee women, but not of the girl who emerges, green-eyed and serious. I could not see the eyes of the refugee women in my dream. This girl steps from the cave like a revelation.

PAUL: The girl steps out into the weeds of the orchard. She is ordinary, her slight legs bruised, her feet bare. She looks to be twelve or so, somewhere between girl and woman. "Speak English," her father says, indicating us with a tilt of the head. She does not speak, but instead does something so beautiful I don't know how to tell it. Or even why it is beautiful. The color rises in her cheeks, and she rushes over to the olive tree and sweeps the three napkins from the branch where they are drying.

BARSANUPHIUS: Yes, she walked over and, on tiptoe, pulled the three napkins down, one at a time, tucked them under her arm, and ran into the cave with them. "I'm sorry," she said when she reemerged. "We are refugees. My mother is dead in the sea, and my father had to help me. I didn't know what to do."

DEMETRIOS: A single chicken runs out of the cave and begins pecking unceremoniously at the dirt around the girl's ankles.

PAUL: She can't be here.

DEMETRIOS: The hen or the girl? Either way, she is here.

BARSANUPHIUS: Perhaps the Blessed Virgin who once rested on these shores has helped this girl—this young woman—who also landed here, to find her way.

ALL: (eyebrows raised)

DEMETRIOS: The father says something in Arabic. She says they'll be gone by nightfall. She's feeling stronger and they will move north. Seeing us stare at the chicken, she says a hawk dropped her in the orchard the day they arrived. She shows them the wound at the back of the chicken's neck.

9. Sleepless Under the Influence

FATHER ACACIUS: At nightfall, word from Karyes has it that the excommunicated brothers across the valley at Esphigmenou are battling it out with the police again. One of the monks is reported to have died when the tractor he was using as a tank overturned and crushed him. This is a lesson for zealots. For heretics.

BARSANUPHIUS: We didn't tell Father Acacius—or Simeon, for that matter—about the napkins, but they both know about the girl. Acacius said she and her father had to go, despite the present dangers. Would we have kept the father alone? We might have, he says.

SIMEON: I seem to be the only one not in thrall to the girl. Or to the she-ness of her. Me and Father Acacius, of course. I didn't give up everything to come to an exclusive retreat where my sister-in-law might show up with a dish to pass like it's a church supper. Call it antifeminism, but it's our brand. The tourists count on it. And we count on them.

BARSANUPHIUS: Avoiding Simeon, who seems to be closing ranks with Acacius now that omelets are out of the question, we pilfer chocolate and spinach pies from the kitchen, as well as a blanket from the storeroom and a little flashlight and a map of Athos. We mark the route so they will avoid Esphigmenou. The bundle finds its way to the orchard before dark.

PAUL: What's happening across the valley keeps us awake at night because we too may be on our way to heresy. Or to dangerous revelation. And who's to say where the difference lies? Strangely, though, the shameful dreams I've had since I was a young man have stopped.

DEMETRIOS: Out in the courtyard, under a gleaming moon, Barsanuphius and I meet with no plan to meet, each of us drawn to the open air where our thoughts and prayers can move freely, which of course, they should do regardless of the cells we choose to live and pray in. Paul wanders out too.

BARSANUPHIUS: Her presence was so ordinary.

DEMETRIOS: And yet even the cloths of her menses fairly glowed in the morning sun.

BARSANUPHIUS: Don't mythologize her. Did you ever have sisters? The cloths didn't glow. But they seemed neutral there. Natural there. Necessary—and not only to her.

PAUL: Yes. But . . . Oh!

DEMETRIOS: It's as if Paul were seeing the burning bush all over again, reliving his wonder over the beautiful act of the "unclean" girl. The spirit expands, does it not? Or maybe he's astonished because he's only now getting it.

PAUL: The spirit expands with the fervor we once applied to excluding her. If, like the zealots across the valley, I am a heretic, I will be a heretic of this wholeness.

DEMETRIOS: What we know we won't stop knowing.

BARSANUPHIUS: But Simeon doesn't know it. For him, if the brotherhood isn't exclusive, it's not a club worth belonging to.

PAUL: And still, the Virgin says *good*. All day for many days, she speaks to us, as garrulous as a girl, when we pray. All day while we recite the Jesus Prayer, asking forgiveness for what we've done and what we have not done, she says *good. Good. Good. Good. Good.* She says she is listening. May she go before them.

BARSANUPHIUS: I wrote the phone number on a bit of paper. My sisters in Romania will help. My father is dead, but my sisters will know what to do. My old country, the country of my heart, is welcoming Syrian refugees at the moment.

DEMETRIOS: The girl was so clumsy I wonder if she wanted us to remember her. I said I would not mythologize her, but I find one of the napkins lying in the field beneath the olive tree. A myth is a truth you don't want to forget.

10. Reliquaries and a Salvo

BARSANUPHIUS: Demetrios is like Cavafy in the poem about the bandages. Only there is nothing sensual about it. Not even anything sacred. Just feminine in a biological sense. Not a wound or a vulnerability or something unclean. It is something we must not fear or despise if we are to live in fullness of spirit. He says we have to remember how that woman-girl troubled the masculine waters of our being here. My sister used to read Rilke. *You must change your life.* Demetrius takes the napkin and hides it.

SIMEON: It's midafternoon. We are at our various labors when a beautiful voice floats through the monastery, down the hallways and into the rooms, then out through the open windows and up the mountainside.

BARSANUPHIUS: The voice of a woman, singing "Ave Maria," not Orthodox but rather a Roman Catholic prayer. It grows from its humble thread to flourish in the stale air of the monastery. It is like cool water drunk slowly after apricot spoon sweets. It is a holy spring surrounded by oleander, or the shade cast by a citrus tree built of sunlight.

SIMEON: It is a manifesto. An opening salvo in a revolution. It's the CD we got as a so-called thank-you gift for a donation to the culturally tone-deaf Refugee Relief Fund.

BARSANUPHIUS: I wander down the hallway toward the source of the music. Along the way, I see Paul wrapping chocolates in the kitchen. He turns as I pass. His face is wet with tears. I think it has been decades since he heard the voice of a woman.

DEMETRIOS: I work all morning with some olive wood and an old pane of glass from the recycling bin. And why should I hide what I am doing? Will I leave it here or take it with me when I am forced to go?

FATHER ACACIUS: Apparently someone found the Barbara Hendricks CD after I put it out with the refuse. Simeon, maybe? Demetrios? My God, I hope the monks over at Esphigmenou don't hear that voice—as sleek as the coat of an animal venturing outside its den alone in moonlight—or that Papist song. Was it Paul? As my chest fills with the mutinous music, I know the damage has been done. Where it started is still unclear. I think, perhaps, with the egg. Or no. The chicken.

PAUL: We all knew the CD went into the trash. Maybe it was Barsanuphius who plucked it out. The voice floods the cavity of my soul as I enter the chapel annex housing all the reliquaries. I feel as though I will burst. The music cuts out abruptly. Father Acacius will have stopped it. Tried to stop it all.

DEMETRIOS: The abrupt edge of the music defines the silence. Unforgettably. There is no ending to it, the music or the silence.

BARSANUPHIUS: I imagine the girl with her father making their way up through the poppy fields and the olive groves of Halkidiki and into the wild mountains of Bulgaria by moonlight. I pray for the kindness of strangers when we, who love the Lord, did not offer refuge. I pray for the refugees to find my sisters. I pray for courage because I'm going to need it in the days ahead. God knows.

PAUL: The wooden icon of my namesake, the Apostle Paul, was found in the sea with an oyster clamped to its forehead hundreds of years ago. Wanting to talk to that one who so earnestly warned of the dangers posed by women, I visit the icon in the hall of the reliquaries. But beside it, in a closed olive wood box, sits a relic that was not there before.

DEMETRIOS: I will surely be sent away when Father Acacius learns what I have done. But what I know, I cannot stop knowing.

PAUL: It seems no more strange and much less stylized than the oyster-bitten icon. It is labeled, in the careful script of Brother Demetrios, *Menstrual Cloth of an Unknown Virgin*, which strikes me as particularly funny because the glass, etched with a snowflake pattern, appears to be left over from the renovation of the lavatory, our most recent improvement. The sound of my own voice laughing is neither mad nor crude but a full and joyous surrender. *Thy will be done*, I say to the God I love. Come what may.

The Inventories

Mustafa lies alone on the ruined mattress among cicada shells and moth wings, on a sheet disintegrated by winter humidity. He stares up at blooms of mold on the ceiling. It is spring at the resort, but the air is still damp in the derelict houses and hotels. A sumac tree has pressed its way up through the middle of the kitchen, and though Mustafa thinks he has been watching for it to happen, it has somehow sprung through the roof without his seeing. Where was he at that moment? Dozing, perhaps. Confusing the dogs of his dream with the feral dogs that roam the streets.

This will be a story about what has already happened. You, too, will be waiting for something more, and there may be a surprise or two along the way, like a rat emerging from a cupboard or a glimpse you get of something as you peer through the chain-link fence dividing the accessible portion of the beach from the forbidden part. But the math that takes place in the form of the inventories is largely aftermath.

In the time before, a woman would have taken the mattress to a balcony or courtyard to dry when the sun came out, coaxing it through the seasons when the tourists were gone. On the wall is a poster of the actress Brigitte Bardot, signed in a loopy hand. It is evening. Mustafa has not kept track of the days, which somehow have become weeks.

The lists of household items he has compiled for the government create the only order within the ruined house he has made his own for the past few days. Lists that were due weeks ago, when he should have been ushered out by the guards one last time, along with the others enlisted by the Turkish authorities. They would have walked down the broken boulevard parallel to the sea, past the showroom full of plaster-dusted 1974 Peugeots and the bakery, toward Famagusta's Old Town, the quarter where he lives.

But in his dream, the tree keeps growing, its branches like keys on an enormous green instrument he would play if only someone would teach him how. He goes from door to door in the abandoned resort looking for someone to teach him. Everyone has gone—except for the soldiers who have made their barracks in a villa near the water.

When he awakens again, a beady-eyed rat is gnawing at his notebook and has reduced the lower corner to shreds. Mustafa throws a shoe at the rat, which moves a few feet off, scampers up onto the countertop, and studies him from behind a metal dishpan.

Wearing a plaid Oxford shirt, Mustafa had set out one Saturday morning in March to work on the inventory and had not returned at dinnertime with the chicken he'd promised Havva he would pick up on his way home. He had worn the same shirt for five or six days before discarding it in the garden of an apartment building and beginning to ransack the bureaus of the dispossessed for a change of clothes.

At first Havva, his wife, might have thought he was merely being unreliable, as he had been pretty much since his mother's death. When he didn't come home with the chicken, she might have opened the refrigerator to look for some hummus, or she would have gone up to the corner cafe for lahmajun. She and Mustafa gave each other space. More and more as time went on. Only by the second or third day of his absence would she, on returning from her work at the university, have begun to think that something had happened to him. But since it seemed no one was out looking for him, she must not have reported him missing. So late in the semester, the principal of the school where he taught would be more angry than concerned.

Mustafa hears the engine of the military jeep a long way off. He has learned to listen for its throaty rumble, which has become part of the circadian rhythm of Varosha. In terms of sound, there is the barking of the feral dogs, who fight over scraps the soldiers throw out, and then the start of the engine when the soldiers make their rounds before sunset. He knows they pass the car showroom and the bakery and the store from which, in the early days after the invasion—the so-called intervention—the wind carried off all of the inflatable beach toys—flamingos and cartoon characters and brightly colored beach balls.

He has kept the inventory for the Turks, who chose him, among others, for the task. Handwritten, it amounts to several thick notebooks he did not submit when the operation was supposedly over. Mustafa supposes that everyone he knows or cares about thinks he went AWOL, especially knowing his attitude toward the Turks. His colleagues and friends would not assume that he had taken his job so very seriously. In fact, Mustafa would have returned to his students, his classes in Turkish and Cypriot history, to thirty-five-minute increments of the storied past, if there were some way to divest himself of all he has taken stock of in the present:

Item#	Description
312	toy guns with caps (one broken, one functional)
313	wool blanket
314	set of Austrian crystal dessert bowls, still in box

315   3 bottles of Drano (special offer?)
316   2 pairs Cretan slippers
317   1 pair Turkish slippers

He was supposed to record anything of value, but in any room he inhabits for even just a few minutes, everything has value. The vanities and the children's sandals, the cooking pots and lemon juicers and linens. He has become laden with the meaningfulness of things. His heart, he thinks, will burst. And he will never have the opportunity to give it all back. If there were a way to lose the birdcages with their piles of feathers and bones, and the wrench sets, and the family photographs, he would have leapt into the street and exposed his presence to the night guard. Even now, he considers doing so. Parked in a lot near the old bakery is a big truck, a Greek-Cypriot moving van with M E T A P H O R A printed on the side. He imagines filling it with the items on his lists, or maybe just the lists themselves, and lumbering out across the barricade, his last moments lived in expectation of a spray of bullets.

Mustafa knows he's gone overboard with the level of detail. For sure, now, they'll know if he drinks one of the bottles of Drano or uses one to poison the dogs. Maybe he writes it all down to save himself from such impulses.

One day, as Mustafa sits at a dining table sorting through a box of war medals and broken jewelry, it occurs to him that Havva was the sort of person who would have seen his disappearance coming even if he hadn't. Considering this possibility, he glances up to see the rat crouched on the kitchen counter, watching him. It returns quickly to the business of compacting the shreds of paper it has scavenged. Mustafa, tired of trying to scare it off, says aloud, "She probably thinks I left her with only the shirt on my back." He hates this thought.

— The plaid one? the rat says.
— Yes.
— Wrong, the rat says. You had the notebook as well. Not to mention pants.
— I wasn't leaving her.
The rat busies itself, casually, with the nest it is building and does not look at him when it says—But maybe you were.
Mustafa has not thought about when he will go back. Preoccupied with the past, he hasn't been looking to the future at all. But something in the powdery sweet air now makes him think of the supple, smooth skin of Havva's shoulders and arms—arms that seemed perfectly suited to whatever task they undertook. He imagines her wearing the emerald-green T-shirt, her green eyes lively but imperturbable as she studies what might seem like his avoidance of her.

On the very day of the Turkish invasion, Mustafa's mother was dying. He'd been caring for her with her ravaged lungs for months. Had been hoisting her up to use the commode and wiping her, then lifting her again in an embrace, on the count of three, to put her back into her chair. He had marveled that excretion was the last of the human needs to be dealt with, and that it did not stop out of any sort of grace or concession to the dying. So consumed was he in that thought and in his labors that he had barely looked up when the neighbors had come over saying the Turks had reached Varosha.

In the days before, the Turks, provoked by the Greeks' attempt to unite Cyprus with Greece, had taken the idyllic harbor of Kyrenia along with many of the northern villages. Mustafa, a Turkish Cypriot, had lived happily alongside his Greek Cypriot neighbors all his life. To him, the Turks were as foreign and unwelcome as they were to the Greek Cypriots.

Mustafa's mother, too, had lived with an open heart. She had turned bitter oranges into spoon sweets and gathered wild greens for her table and the tables of local tavernas in winter. There was a joy in her that was Mustafa's primary source of awe, worn thin as he was by his work at the high school. The history he taught, full of conflict between East and West, Christian and Muslim, weighed on him, as did his students' hormone-driven distractedness.

He understood now that a single grief, full-blown, was really all a body and a heart were capable of. It was like a house destroyed by a small central explosion that would not, then, be shaken by any aftershock, even if that shock were somehow of greater magnitude.

Each morning after his mother's death, as he sat at the table drinking his coffee, Havva touched the back of his neck and asked how he was feeling. He always said he was fine. It was what he thought she wanted to hear. But each day a little more distance opened between them until they were moving in spheres almost completely separate. He had married Havva because she would not replace his mother in his affections but would occupy a different space altogether in his universe. Havva was sensuous, serious, not much of a cook. A marine biologist, she taught at the university. She was someone who always knew there was a dark underside to the blue-sky world. Mustafa, on the other hand, even with fair warning, had been broadsided by his mother's passing. Perhaps he was ashamed for Havva to see how it devastated him. How ill-equipped he was for even the losses that were inevitable. Not to mention the ones that weren't.

The labor of documentation has begun to drift away from the objects of the dispossessed into days and weeks Mustafa feels he must record. He is living on preserved bitter oranges (like the ones his mother used to make), pickled beans, olives, and Nutella. It pains him to consume the stores of what someone else laid up for a future that was abruptly canceled. So he makes a ritual of opening the jars and releasing the hopes under their lids. He eats in remembrance of those who fled. He gathers wild greens and picks oranges and lemons from the trees in the gardens. Also capers, which know how to grow only in the wild. He cures them first in a little jar with salt. For protein, he eats the eggs of a chicken from Famagusta that he has coaxed to lay near the chain-link and concertina fence. One afternoon while scavenging, he finds a rusty petrol can in the garage of a block of flats. He empties its contents into the tank of the METAPHORA truck.

Sometimes, though already it seems too late to merely wander back, he imagines returning home. He knows what Havva would say. "I think you've been depressed, Mustafa." "It's called grief, Havva," he would tell her. "You don't have to agree with me," she'd say.

— What if she's right? the rat says.

— What do you know? Mustafa says, looking over at the rat, which seems to have gotten at more of his paper somehow and is mixing it with human hair to make a nest at the corner of the countertop, in plain view.

— I'm just saying. What if you're a depressed derelict obsessing over memorabilia?

— Think of me as a poet. This is my elegy. And you're reducing it to a rat's nest.

— Get over it.

— OK then, an anthropologist.

In a cultural history, you would read things like, "A resident of Famagusta owned five small sacks of *lana de cambelon* and sixty sacks of goat hair," followed by the observation, "The names of the two fiber types and the distinction between them . . . imply that neither ordinary sheep's wool nor ordinary goat hair entered into Cypriot camlet weave." But Mustafa knows that the Turkish authorities have no interest in anthropology. The type of inventory they have requisitioned is just something one does when in power—a demonstration of authority. Or it would be for purposes of taxation (though there was no one left to tax in Varosha), or just to revel in the spoils of war.

Mustafa fills his head with lists as he lingers, vagrant, in the ruins—mostly unofficial lists these days. He has imagined people's arguments at dinner and their interrupted loves. Their infidelities. Their business successes and their homework, completed reluctantly in the leafy courtyards. Their prayers and their dancing. He has lost time to living so many lives. The lives he imagines are those of Greek Cypriots, who were Christians. He himself is Muslim, though only nominally.

One afternoon, he writes down what he remembers of the charges brought against the Knights Templar by the Bishop of Famagusta in 1310—charges also perhaps imagined:

XI   That these brothers sometimes trampled upon that cross
XII   That they sometimes urinated on or made others urinate on that cross and several times did this on Good Friday
XIII That some of them on that day or on another of Holy Week were accustomed to meet together for the aforesaid trampling and urinating
XIV   That they adored a certain cat which appeared to them at their meeting.

Mustafa doubts that the knights were guilty of these things—as charged by men of their own faith. He himself cares little for the cross, but he urinates in the garden and does not adore the cats he lives among. They are filthy and when once or twice in his loneliness he petted one, he found he had contracted worms.

He wanders the rooms of the abandoned hotels, taking the keys from where they hang behind the desk, and sometimes, seduced by the intimate lives of others, he masturbates by moonlight. All day, he is making inventories. Today, he takes stock of the reasons he has not left the quarter.

1. He would have to give account for his prolonged absence.
2. Havva would by now have become accustomed to not having to remind him of things—everyday things like the grocery list or a visit to the barber.
3. He is a profiteer living on what his Greek Cypriot neighbors, now forcefully relocated to Paralimni or Larnaca, have left behind.
4. He has no idea whether or not it is Good Friday, or if any day can be good without foreboding.

One list morphs into another, brutally detailed histories and collective traumas mingled with causes for personal guilt, all of it straining toward whatever it is that he has missed. A reason not to kill himself. Because nothing will surprise him now. Mustafa even makes an inventory of the things that would not. He discusses the possibilities with the rat, who surprises him by turning up at a different moment each day. Same beady-eyed industry.

The rat, gnawing on a pair of two-year-dirty panties or a sack of fava flour, says—Suppose the British pulled out of the EU?

It says—What if your mother-in-law embezzled money from the coffers of the Lala Mustafa Pasha mosque?

Unearthing some white asparagus bulbs, the rat suggests—The seawater will rise so high it will lap at the oven in the abandoned bakery.

— Yes, Mustafa says. Yes, yes, yes. It probably will.

— You will soon be required to cook your neighbor's femur in a stew to prove your loyalty.

Well, the rat doesn't say that. Mustafa dreams that one and can't eat even a boiled egg for days. He feels as if he's swallowed a stone.

— What if you did swallow a stone? says the rat.

What doesn't surprise us makes us duller and more passive, and what doesn't kill us merely leaves us waiting to die. This is what Mustafa has come to believe.

But then the belly dancer appears one night around dusk on the flat roof of a building just outside the dead zone—undulating but not womanly, more taut than supple, his shape flat against the sky. The music is the same music you'd expect. The dancing isn't a parody but rather is lovely in its hermaphroditic way at almost-night just beyond the concertina.

Mustafa takes pleasure in the belly dancer's appearance, and it is this pleasure that surprises him. His ability to feel it. Still. Then the music disappears abruptly with the boom box down an unseen staircase.

The rat says—The Georgians are using the moon as a garbage dump.

Mustafa says—And nobody even knows we're here.

Mustafa records a leaky sunrise over the eastern Mediterranean and the mud-rain that the wind brings, carrying dust from the Sahara. It spatters the broken panes of windows and dirt-washes the abandoned cars. There is so much drama if you only sit still long enough to see it—lizards devouring flies, ants carrying twigs to build their fungal gardens, weeds breaking stone. He has stopped getting the news except in fragments from the radio of the military jeep—and it's always declarations of political intractability. But as long as the soldiers keep their patrol, he can assume the rat is telling him all he needs to know.

Nights on the rooftop, the belly dancer works his bowel and his rib cage like a snake that has swallowed a rat. The rat is himself. His own stomach and intestine. It's all done with exquisite control. He shifts the cage of his ribs like a courtesan carrying the bird of her own freedom to and fro on a balcony in a harem. His arms swarm the graying sky—counter motion to the white and gray dust. He quivers and jangles, and Mustafa watches him each evening, imagining that if he were to send a postcard to the world, it would be this dance.

Mustafa moves every three or four days so as not to create much evidence of himself. The rat follows him. No matter. Mustafa buries his own shit, which resembles the pellets of a wild or constipated dog. He is ruminating on the sound the locusts make. He has been watching them grate their legs together and is taking refuge in this one evening while opening a can of white beans when he hears the sound of the military jeep's radio passing outside the apartment where he is holed up. *Yesterday the Turkish army, in brash defiance of liberal European Union* . . . Nothing new. While he isn't paying attention, the rat scurries over and knocks the can of beans out of his hand. It clatters on stone. Now the radio lingers and is interrupted by the two soldiers on duty talking to one another.

Will anything surprise you now?

What if one of the soldiers steps into the courtyard with the broad beam of a military-issue flashlight and empties a round of ammo from his semiautomatic. Then he shrugs, says to his comrade, "Nothing, I guess." Mustafa, having buried himself in the massive geranium that has taken over the eastern end of the garden, recognizes in this brief sequence of events and in the soldier's appraisal of it, the history of the world. When the soldiers leave, he sees the white-feathered body lying beside the chain-link fence where it took the spray. His chicken.

What Mustafa loads into the truck that night: forty bales of misery and failed diplomacy, a burden of disappointed hopes, the camel hair shirt of his regret, a fine-tooth comb for picking nits, a wool blanket, a few rounds of wistful sighs and protests, a catalog of dreams, the explosives of his stored-up anger—enough to blow the local government buildings sky high—and a dozen apologies to Havva for all that is wrong with his decision. Also, a pair of the woolen slippers from Crete. He's not sure whether what he's doing is insurrection, martyrdom, protest, surrender, or just plain suicide.

He thinks, tonight, that he recognizes the dancer. It's a kid from his class in Ottoman history. The boy always seemed to disbelieve Mustafa, though Mustafa didn't understand how that was possible when it was history he was teaching. Things had happened. You couldn't argue with that. Mustafa was teaching about the decline of the Ottoman Empire, but that boy said the empire didn't decline. He argued change didn't necessarily mean decline. And there he was, on the roof, himself a kind of argument against what felt like the end of the world. Maybe he would say it wasn't.

Mustafa has always had a hard time weighing personal trouble against the larger troubles—shared troubles. He can't tell the difference, say, between his grief over his mother's death and all of the losses of all of the refugees from Varosha. Or between knowledge of his own mortality and what feels like the impending death of civilization. Or at least *a* civilization. And maybe even, eventually, the world. He knows the instinct for survival of the species runs in his veins, though somehow he feels that the inventories could easily dissolve into the species' silence. There is a peacefulness about ruin—the death of expectation—that makes him want to lie down quietly and surrender on behalf of humanity. Is he half mad? Sometimes he wants only to let the cicadas and the overgrowth of misdeeds cover him and all of us together.

But there on the rooftop is the boy—the one who used to argue about the Ottoman Empire and who now seems to have taken all the contortions that living in this world demands and turned them to fluidity and movement against the night sky. Mustafa climbs into the truck.

You think this can't end well. Or if it does, it will not be realistic. Yet what you probably wish for, as Mustafa puts the truck in gear and rolls it first backward then forward down the avenue, is a triumph of the heart, a repurposing of testosterone and ego, a crossing over into a zone that is free of the absurd waste that conflict and aggression have circumscribed. And why shouldn't you have what you wish for?

Mustafa's gaining speed in the M E T A P H O R A and is headed straight for the northern gate. You imagine men and women somewhere at the table of peaceful negotiation, about to make a breakthrough. All four tires as flat as humility, Mustafa's rolling on metal like rail stock across the broken concrete streets. Can you think some soldier was distracted and forgot to close the gate? Or that the game's so old there's no one standing guard? How much is riding on these threads of hope!

Mustafa busts through the concrete barricade, tearing off the chain-link gate too before the truck gives up in a puff of exhaust and comes to a halt about ten meters outside the border. It is silent, except for the hiss of the radiator. Mustafa is curiously aware of the absence of gunfire. He is, in fact, not dead. Can the Turkish military be gone? He descends from the cab and looks down the road to the newest hotel at the open end of the beach—the first place outside the chain link and concertina. No doormen or SUVs or taxis. No vendor in the little market on the other side of the road leading back toward the Old Town.

It seems that something has swept the rest of the city and there is nobody left. Mustafa walks to the water's edge and dips a wary hand into the bright sea lapping at his feet. He spots a few empty trash bags floating in the shallow bay, dark blobs in a blue-green expanse. Have the Turks finally drilled their way to war with the Greeks in the exclusive economic zone Cyprus claims? Has everyone been evacuated on account of a chemical spill?

It occurs to Mustafa, as the waves lap at the empty beach, that while he has been mourning his mother's passing and then taking in all the sadness of the absent refugees, something more has erased the life that once was. Even the gulls are quiet along the road to Famagusta. Each day makes it clear that he was merely naive the day before. He has fallen behind in his griefs.

And why is he still carrying the dead chicken? He wanders cautiously along the road toward the Old Town, where his own house is. Has there been a wildfire? He smelled smoke for a couple of days a while back, and there is a small patch of scorched pines near the stadium, but nothing to explain the vacancy of the city. He wonders if he might be breathing noxious fumes, invisible gases from some accident.

Eerily now, the air is filling with dust, coming up from Africa and causing a brown haze to settle over everything. This is not unusual, except in its intensity.

A man loves his mother, who has a heart as big as the wind. She means the world to him. He loses her. Then he loses the world. There must be a difference between a civic, communal grief and an apocalyptic one, but something inside him that should calibrate these things and tell him how to respond is broken. Maybe he has been trying to fix it.

Turning to look back just once before walking in the direction of home, he sees a figure out on the beach, closer to the chain-link barrier and an empty guard tower. One lonely figure that stands between him and the idea of apocalypse. The figure is bent, examining something in the sand. It is late afternoon, and the air has grown dim and hazy with the African dust. You can't feel it on your skin yet, but you can see it. He stops, cautious, and watches her straighten up and throw off a shirt or a jacket. It is a woman.

Mustafa experiences a shock of recognition at the splash of emerald green revealed against the dull sky.

He hurries over, past the observation tower, his heels sinking deep into the sand. He skirts two mounded areas staked off with string. He is very near when the woman stops what she is doing and looks up to see him. Perfectly still, she watches him approach. He knows it is her, though she has changed—the hair she brushes from her face now visibly silvering, the lines around her mouth deeper. He doesn't think about how he might have changed—the full beard, the tourist shirt. "Havva!" he shouts, his voice full of wonder and trepidation.

She looks at him for a long moment before gesturing to the dead chicken he still carries in his right hand.

How long, he wonders, has he been gone? She looks like a woman of fifty, though she was considerably younger when he left home. Was Varosha some kind of time warp? And then, smiling slightly at how mad he must look, he says, "I guess you've made something else for dinner."

She laughs in a single, weary, closed-mouth syllable.

"Havva," he says, "I know I've got a lot to explain, and I'm not sure I can explain it, but what happened here? Where is everybody?"

Her hands resting on her hips, she surveys the landscape. "I guess we should go in reverse, since I don't remember exactly where we were when you left." She picks up a mallet and begins tap-tapping at a wooden stake she has poked into the sand. "People were just returning to their houses," *tap, tap* "to repair the damage after the wildfires swept the northern quarter of the city—worst fires in two hundred years," *tap, tap, tap.* "Then the cruise ship came into harbor bringing with it the pandemic. As you can see, the dust storms—" But she stopped and studied him. "Where have you been, Mustafa?"

She picks up another stake and begins tapping at it in rhythms that sound, against the blank beachscape, like Morse code. For trouble. He watches her face for any sign of resentment toward him and does not find it, though he knows she must feel it.

"Varosha," he says.

"I guess you knew about the dust then?" she says. "But maybe not that it's picking up toxic airborne pollutants and bringing them here from North Africa, causing lots of asthma. But the virus, which also affects the lungs—that seems to have originated in China."

"Is everyone dead?"

"Under lockdown until further notice."

"But you're out," he says. He puts the chicken down in the sand. It is good for nothing now anyway. Or maybe it could be boiled. How long has he been carrying it? It feels, suddenly, like years.

"I gave myself permission," she says.

He raises an eyebrow.

"And paid the military police," she adds. She seems to be reflecting on that decision.

"To let you do what?"

"The sea turtles have returned," she says, suddenly animated. "The lights have been out a long while now, and they've come back to nest."

"I was in there, Havva. You may not believe me, but I was working on the inventory. I just couldn't stop tallying the losses. I didn't want to go on as if it hadn't happened. I felt, in there, like the last man on earth."

Havva reties her hair since the wind has picked up and is batting it at her cheek. She says, "The rest of us were still out here though."

Ah. There it is.

A couple of gulls pick at a broken eggshell nearby. "And by the way, I have never not believed you. Should I have come after you? It's just that I thought—I knew you weren't dead. But I knew I could never give you enough space."

He weighs the virtue in telling her what he tells her next. "An hour ago, I drove out through the barricade in plain sight, expecting to be shot. But after I got through, I found . . . Where is the military?"

"They were moved over to Famagusta to enforce the lockdown. No one's allowed to leave the house except to get supplies. And yes, people are dying. Some people have died."

They are both quiet for a while as Havva ties a string around the stakes to protect the mound of eggs. "They started to hatch last night," she says. "The moon guides them back to the water."

"What did you do with the lists? The inventory?" she asks.

He gasps, and then begins to laugh and keeps laughing until he collapses on his knees in the sand. Havva can't help laughing with him when she says, "Mustafa? You forgot them, Mustafa?"

He is crying now. "Oh my God! They're still in there. Sheaves of them!"

Havva moves toward him, and he puts his arms around her knees and makes her fall into the sand—away from the turtle's nest. He crawls over to her head, and she touches his hair and his wet cheek where the beard takes over his face. He kisses her, and it seems miraculous that he is still alive enough to love the grit on her lips and the salt air he can taste there too. He wishes he had his pen and his notebook to write down the good things that still surprise him. Number one: Havva. Number two: Havva's arms. Number three: Havva's arms digging and tapping their codes.

She releases him. Rising to her feet again, she says, "One or two small things, Mustafa. That's all we can do. We'll help them follow the moonlight. And then we'll go home. We can talk about all of this later. Look at the sky! It's crazy!" The sand arrives in a dust they can feel on their skin.

Mustafa stands up and touches her with a tenderness he has not felt in years. "You must have needed things while I was gone. I'm sorry, Havva. I lost track of time. I made you go it alone."

She says nothing. And he truly has no idea how much time has slipped away. He can't bear to ask.

Now, at dusk, they watch what at first looked like trash bags floating in the bay begin to make their way ashore. Some adult turtles, the late arrivals, Havva explains, are just now coming in to nest, while the eggs laid a couple of months ago, in late March or early April, have begun to hatch.

The dust settles on their shirts and the backs of their necks and in their hair. They start walking home, but Mustafa turns and looks back, worried. "Will they be OK?" he asks, feeling the gritty mass of his beard with both hands. "The little ones?"

"Sand they can manage. There are other things that will get most of them before they mature. Many of them tomorrow morning, even. Gulls. Snapper. Crabs. Raccoons. But look at this one, coming ashore." She points. They watch the marvelous reptile move in her scaly armor, her eyelids heavy, like endurance, like the centuries lumbering on, carrying their great weight ashore, arriving at the land of opportunity.

"I think you've been depressed, Mustafa."

"It's called grief, Havva," he says, his hand dropping to his side.

"You don't have to agree with me. It's just what I see."

"You sound like a high school student reading Kafka. They always came to my class right after World Literature. Couldn't believe how depressed that guy was. By the way, do you also think the Ottoman Empire never really—"

"Shhh," she says, putting a finger to his sandy lips. "Enough," she says. "Let's go home."

In the middle of the sandy beach at their backs is a lifeguard stand you've barely noticed until a quick movement there catches your eye: a bald, pink tail disappearing up inside the ladder. The rat reappears on the seat of the stand and darts to the edge, where it lingers.

— You don't believe this ending, do you? it says, taunting.

— Why shouldn't I?

The rat's eyes are shining when it says—Their moment of happiness is undeserved. Seriously. They're laughing? Things will only get worse. One of them will die soon, probably.

— I can still be surprised. And what about the belly dancer?

The rat says—What about him?

— It's evening. I'm waiting for Mustafa to show her.

Acknowledgments

Many thanks to the journals in which these stories originally appeared: *Cincinnati Review* for "The Girl Who Loved Boyan Slat," *Kenyon Review* for "The Dalai Lama's Smile," *Nimrod International Journal* for "The Inventories," *Ploughshares* for "The Slight," and *Southern Review* for "The Intervention" (under the title "Appointment on the Bhagsu Road"). Thanks, too, to the National Endowment for the Arts for the Fellowship in Fiction that enabled me to finish this collection.

The quoted material regarding Cypriot inventories in "The Inventories" is taken from David Jacoby's "Camlet Manufacture, Trade in Cyprus, and the Economy of Famagusta from the Thirteenth to the Late Fifteenth Century" in *Medieval and Renaissance Famagusta*, ed. Michael J. K. Walsh et al. The partial list of charges against the Knights Templar in the same story is taken verbatim from Anne Gilmour-Bryson's *The Trial of the Templars in Cyprus*.

Heartfelt appreciation to those who offered their literary perceptions along the way: Robert Rosenberg, without whose instigation these stories would not have happened; Joe Scapellato, whose enthusiasm and engagement with the text always made me want to go back at it; Jim Buck, my forever literary companion and trusted reader; Kat Lecky, for her sharp commentary from a critic's perspective; Shara McCallum, ever generous literary friend and reader; Martha Vaccarella, whose well-exercised readerly instinct I trust; Emily Nemens and Caitlin Horrocks, both exacting editors who helped the stories they published find their final forms; and Magdalini Thoma, Mustafa Kurt, and Cathy Emery, for their astute cultural checks. Thanks to my friends in Cyprus and Greece, and to the people I met in India, all of whom gave me access to the complexity of their worlds. Most especially, thanks to my editor, Nicola Mason, for bringing this book into the world with insight, expertise, and care.